SEDUCED BY A LADY'S HEART

D1564346

SEDUCED BY A LADY'S HEART

Christi Caldwell

Copyright © 2015 by Christi Caldwell

All rights reserved. No part of this book may be reproduced in any form by any electronic or mechanical means—except in the case of brief quotations embodied in critical articles or reviews—without written permission.

The characters and events portrayed in this book are fictitious. Any similarity to real persons, living or dead, is purely coincidental and not intended by the author.

License Notes
This book is licensed for your personal enjoyment only. This book may not be re-sold or given away to other people. If you would like to share this book with another person, please purchase an additional copy for each recipient. If you're reading this book and did not purchase it or borrow it, or it was not purchased for your use only, then please return it and purchase your own copy. Thank you for respecting the hard work of the author.
For more information about the author:

For more information about the author:
christicaldwellauthor@gmail.com
www.christicaldwellauthor.com

ISBN: 1519140592
ISBN-13: 9781519140593

DEDICATION

To Rory
My beautiful boy. With the Lords of Honor series being about
heroes and soldiers, there is no one who deserves this dedication
more than you—my strong, courageous warrior in all things. You
inspire me with your strength and humble me with your beautiful spirit, in the face of great challenges. *You* are my hero.

ACKNOWLEDGEMENTS

To Katie

Thank you for wanting to read Lieutenant Jones' story as much as I wanted to tell it. I connected with Jones from the moment he was staring blankly out the window during Lady Emmaline's visit in "Forever Betrothed, Never the Bride". The day I came onto Facebook and read your post asking to know his story, was a wonderful day!

ONE

London, England
Spring, 1819

I n all of Lady Eloise Yardley, the Countess of Sherborne's, twenty-eight years she could likely place the underhanded, questionable things she'd done on one hand. And that unimpressive list of sins included stealing another girl's peppermints when she'd been a girl of seven.

Her palms dampened under the unease churning in her belly, and to still her trembling fingers she dusted her palms along the sides of her silver, satin skirts. Staring at the modest, marble foyer of London Hospital, Eloise acknowledged that this disloyal act was far worse than stealing peppermints.

"My lady, if you'd rather not visit, it is more than understandable," the older nurse's words snapped into her musings.

Startled into movement, Eloise slapped a hand to her chest. "Er, no. I'm quite all right," she lied. She cleared her throat. "I'm merely…" *Terrified. Nauseous. Panicked.* And every emotion in between at the prospect of striding down those corridors and entering the sterile rooms of the hospital.

The gentle light in the woman's eyes indicated she'd detected the lie.

Eloise sighed. "Shall we?"

The nurse's white eyebrows shot to her hairline in apparent surprise and then an approving glint replaced her earlier concern. She gave a brief nod. "If you'll follow me," she murmured.

The older woman didn't attempt to fill the awkward pall of silence, for which Eloise was grateful. She didn't imagine she could muster a single, coherent thought. She furrowed her brow. A matter she'd have to rectify if this carefully orchestrated visit went to plan. She eyed the dreary, white walls, the hard plaster devoid of cheer and life. Then, life had taught her early on that nothing ever truly went to plan.

"I am always so grateful to see ladies such as yourself taking time to visit the wounded soldiers," Nurse Maitland said.

Their footsteps fell into a synchronized rhythm.

Guilt stabbed at Eloise. She'd never felt more ashamed than she did in that moment. For it was not strictly altruistic reasons that brought her into this feared place. Just the opposite, really. Remorse kept her silent.

"Lady Drake, the Marchioness of Drake, has long visited the hospital."

She'd, of course, known that. "Has she?" Eloise's voice emerged as a high-pitched squeak, which earned a sideways glance from the woman.

"Indeed. In fact, she is here even n—oh, my! Are you all right, my lady?"

Eloise stumbled and, unfortunately for the older nurse, caught herself using the woman's tall, narrow frame. "Yes," she replied, lamely. Mortified heat burned her cheeks. However, the thrill of excitement coursed through her, more powerful than any small emotion of embarrassment. So, the marchioness was here. She quickly yanked her hands back from Nurse Maitland's narrow, but seemingly capable, shoulders. "Pardon me," she said belatedly.

The woman passed a concerned glance over her face and then resumed walking. Eloise kept pace alongside her. With each step drawing her closer to those dreaded hospital rooms, panic pounded in her chest. It flared hot and strong until the familiar buzzing filled her ears and she blinked back the black dots that flecked her vision.

Nurse Maitland said something, her words lost to the memories churning at an agonizingly quick pace through her mind. The older woman looked to Eloise with a smile, her unheard words clearly

2

merited a like response and so she told her mind to tell her lips to move. She mustered a weak, clearly sufficient smile for the woman continued on.

Since the dark days, as she'd come to refer to them, she'd detested any and all things pertaining to illness—hospitals, doctors, the color white, the heat of a fever. All of it. It was irrational and insensible and she'd never been accused of being either irrational or insensible. But there you had it.

"Ah, here we are," the nurse murmured.

And here she was. The last place in the world she cared to be. Feet twitching with the urge to flee, Eloise swallowed past the enormous swell of fear in her throat and stared at the double doors. Yet a place she had come…*for him.* Finding strength in the memory of him, even as that was all he lived as—a fleeting memory of her past—she drew in a steadying breath.

Nurse Maitland, unaware of Eloise's inner turmoil, opened a door and motioned her forward.

Eloise hesitated and craned her head inside the doorway and blinked. The cheerful room with rows of beds was nothing one would conjure when they imagined the dreary walls of a lonely hospital. Extravagant blooms in generous vases lent a merry feel to the room. Which was ludicrous, of course. There could never truly be anything joyous in this room, filled with men who'd sacrificed so much, received so little, and, no doubt, forgotten by all. Nay, not all. Most. She swallowed hard at the sight of the men confined to these beds.

Again, guilt pricked her conscience. For her reason in being here was not the honorable, admirable sort.

He had been one of them.

Oh, God. *Why didn't I know?* But more…*Why didn't you tell me?* She would have braved the horrors she'd carried all these years just to step through the doors and see him.

Because you never mattered, a silent voice reminded her, pragmatic and sincere.

"Ahem." Eloise forced her legs to move forward as the nurse discreetly cleared her throat. She stepped inside, not knowing what she expected. The room to suddenly burn with the heat of bodies ablaze with fever? The scent of vomit and sweat that even the mere memory of caused bile to build in her throat? She swallowed it forcibly back and walked alongside Nurse Maitland.

She glanced about at the soldiers, still confined to these beds. Many eyed her with blank, empty stares. Others with a modicum of curiosity in their bored gazes. Eloise managed a smile and then continued surveying the room.

And then found *her*. She froze.

The young woman, a diminutive, smallish figure with brown hair the color of chocolate sat beside a gentleman, her head bent over a book as she read. Forgetting all the rules of propriety drilled into her from early on, Eloise studied the Marchioness of Drake.

Nurse Maitland continued on and then realized Eloise no longer fell into step beside her, for she turned back with a frown. She followed her gaze fixed on the young lady. "Ah, forgive me. Are you acquainted with Her Ladyship?"

"No," Eloise's response was instantaneous. After all, she couldn't very well admit that she'd never really been welcomed into the same social circles as the respectable marchioness, daughter of a duke. Unlike Eloise who'd been a mere knight's daughter, who'd captured the notice of the Earl of Sherborne. In truth, however, Eloise well knew she could have coordinated a meeting with the woman at a place other than London Hospital. But it was a need to know not only this woman, but more importantly this place.

As though feeling her stare, the marchioness glanced up from her reading and looked about. Her gaze collided with Eloise. A wide smile wreathed the woman's face and she lifted a hand in greeting.

Some of the anxiety went out of Eloise as she managed her first real smile and she returned the gesture.

"Please, allow me to introduce you."

For the first time in so very long, excitement stirred to life inside her as, with each passing step, her fear of this room, of her plans, of simply being here slipped away. Oh, they didn't disappear altogether, but rather remained muted by the hope in her heart.

"Lady Drake," the nurse said with far more familiarity than Eloise expected as they drew to a stop beside a gentleman's bed.

Eloise glanced down and, for a fleeting moment, her reasons for seeking out the marchioness faded when paired with the extreme starkness in the blond-haired, blue-eyed gentleman's empty eyes.

"Nurse Maitland," the marchioness returned.

The remainder of her words was lost as Eloise rudely met the gaze of a stranger who stared boldly back. Pain tightened her belly while she replaced this stranger's face with another. Is this what Lucien had become? She'd never imagined the gentle, polite young boy she'd considered a friend anything but full of laughter and cheer.

Then, if he were still that laughing, cheerful man wouldn't he have returned? a voice needled.

"This is Lady Sherborne." Nurse Maitland's greeting jerked her back.

She flushed. "M-my lady," she stammered and dropped a belated curtsy.

The marchioness rose in a flurry of skirts. She waved a hand breezily about. "Oh, please, there is no need for such formality," she assured. "Emmaline will suffice." She smiled, again a grin teeming with warmth and sincerity. "We do so enjoy the addition of new, pleasant guests, isn't that correct, Lieutenant Forbes?"

His lips quirked up in half a grin. "Aye." For a moment Eloise wondered if she'd merely imagined his earlier coolness. Then he shifted his attention to her and the wary mistrust replaced all hint of warmth.

Eloise shifted upon her feet, feeling like an interloper in this world. In all worlds, really. But for the meadows of Kent, she'd never really felt a kindred connection to any place.

"…Just showing Lady Sherborne about…"

She wet her lips, torn with the purpose that had brought her here and this sudden need to see the men who called this hospital home. Lucien was once one of them. Agony twisted her belly into knots. With a slow nod she said, "It was a pleasure meeting you, my…Emmaline," she quickly amended at the gentle reproach in the marchioness' eyes.

"Indeed," Emmaline concurred. She lifted a hand in parting and returned her attention to Lieutenant Forbes.

With pained reluctance, she fell into step beside Nurse Maitland once again. "The gentlemen enjoy when books are read to them. They enjoy singing," she said with a wave of her hand about the room.

Eloise winced. She couldn't imagine a more egregious affront than to visit these men and torture them with the off-key, high whine of her singing voice. "I do not have any books with me," she said, regret filling her. Now, she wished she'd been less selfish. Wished she'd stopped to consider there were men much like Lucien, alone, dependent upon the charity of strangers for every kindness. Agony knifed through her at the idea of him alone at this hospital when there had been others who loved him, waiting for him. *There was me. I was there.*

Nurse Maitland stopped beside the bed of a tall, broad bear of a man with shocking white-blond hair. She gave her an encouraging smile. "Just your presence alone is welcome," she assured. She didn't allow Eloise to issue protestations, but turned instead to the gentleman with his gaze fixed on the window. "Lieutenant-Captain Washburn," the nurse greeted.

He inclined his head in greeting. "Nurse Maitland." The broad stranger shifted his attention to Eloise.

"Allow me to introduce Lady Sherborne. She is so good as to visit." Guilt twisted Eloise's belly. There was a self-serving purpose to her being here that didn't merit the nurse's kindness. With a parting smile for Eloise that only magnified Eloise's sense of guilt, Nurse Maitland took her leave.

Panic budded inside Eloise's chest at the idea of being alone, in this room, though, she wasn't truly alone. She took a steadying breath and concentrated on that saving fact.

"Are you all right, my lady?" Lieutenant-Captain Washburn asked, concern in his question.

What a weak ninny everyone must take her to be. She mustered a smile. "I am," she assured as he motioned to the small, wooden chair behind her. Eloise perched on the edge of the hard, uncomfortable seat. Thought better of it and dragged it closer to the side of his bed.

They took each other in for a long while, eyeing each other in silence. "Are you certain you are—?"

She slashed the air with a hand. "Quite." She paused and a thick blanket of tense silence fell. Then, she'd never been the loquacious sort, unable to fill all voids of silence as Miss Sara Abbott could. Eloise fisted her skirts at the unwitting reminder of the lovely golden-blonde woman, the vicar's flawlessly perfect daughter who'd moved into the village following the previous vicar's death. Sara would know what to say. Eloise, however, never did. And for that, she broke into the awkward pause with truth. "I'm nervous at hospitals." By the slight widening of his eyes, she gathered she'd shocked him with her bold admission. She turned her attention out the window. "They remind me of illness," she said, more to herself.

"I'm sorry, my lady."

She caught the inside of her lower lip between her teeth and returned her attention to him. "I imagine you'd be a good deal better with no company than my miserable self," she said with a wry smile.

"No," he hastened to assure. "Not a good deal better. Perhaps just a bit better." He winked.

A startled bark of laughter escaped her, earning the curious stares of those around her. And with a glib comment and a wink, all the remaining tension left her body. "Thank you," she said softly.

"Smiling is important, my lady," he said sagely. "Even when the memories creep in."

She started. How did he—?

"You wear it in your face, my lady." The astute stranger jerked his chin in her direction and reflexively Eloise touched her cheeks. "I imagine we all do."

She wore it in her entire being. Eloise dropped her hands to her lap. Regrets of the past, the agony of her failures. "How long have you been here?" she asked quietly.

His lips twisted wryly. "More years than I care to remember." Her heart twisted with regret for his loneliness. An image flashed to mind of Lucien, here, with these men for friends and company. Had he spoken of his past? Had he spoken of her?

As soon as the silly musing slipped in, it disappeared. Lucien would have never made mention of a girlhood friend, even as she'd loved him, his heart had belonged to Sara. Again, the guilt of her failings pebbled in her belly. "I'm sorry," she said at last.

He stiffened, a proud man who'd never welcome or accept pity.

"Not for your situation, Lieutenant-Captain." She'd already received heaps more of the wasted emotion than she could ever want. "I would never pity you or anyone else for their life." She'd never dare subject someone to that unwelcome, useless sentiment. "But I'm sorry you are in a place you'd rather not be, because I know the regret of... that."

Sunlight slashed through the window and cast his bed in a soft glow. She followed the beam out the crystal pane, hating that regrets had crept in with their tentacle-like grip.

"Forgive me," he apologized, jerking her attention back. "It was unfair of me to make assumptions about your experiences." A small chuckle rumbled up from his chest. "Life's experiences should have certainly taught me better," he said with a small grin.

"It's not always easy to remember." From the corner of her eye she spied the slender woman at the opposite end of the room, stand and start for the door. Conflict warred within as she was besieged by a desire to stay and speak with the gentleman and the urge to fly across the room and stop the woman she'd come here with the express intention of seeking out.

The soldier motioned to Lady Drake.

"Are you—?"

"Quite certain," he assured her.

"Forgive me." With a hasty whisper of apologies and a promise to return, she raced across the room, earning more and more curious stares.

Satin slippers proved a disastrous selection for her day's attire. She cried out as she slid like a skater upon ice and collided into the marchioness' back. Lady Drake pitched forward and would have toppled onto her face if Eloise didn't steady her about the shoulders.

Emmaline spun around, a warm, grateful smile on her face. "Oh, my, why thank you very much. I do believe I would have made quite a cake of myself right here."

Eloise waved off the unnecessary expression of gratitude. "No, my lady…Emmaline," she amended when the kindly woman opened her mouth. "It was—"

"Please say you'll join me for tea, my lady."

…Entirely Eloise's fault. "Please, just Eloise," she blurted.

The marchioness' smile widened. "Splendid! Shall we say tomorrow?" With a quick curtsy she spun on her heel and marched from the room, leaving Eloise staring wide-eyed after her.

Well…that was indeed a good deal easier than she'd imagined it would be.

TWO

Lucien Jones moved with military precision through the palatial townhouse of his employer, the Marquess of Drake. The stiff cravat threatened to choke him and he tugged at the blasted fabric. An ache so potent it was a physical force filled him with longing for the comfort he'd known in the marquess' stables.

"Bloody cravats," he mumbled and a wide-eyed scullery maid scurried in the opposite direction. At one time he would have felt a modicum of shame for scaring the staff. That proper gentleman was gone. Long dead. He tightened his jaw and paused outside his employer's office. He raised a hand.

"Enter," Lord Drake's voice broke through the wood panel before he'd even knocked.

He pressed the handle. "You wanted to see me, Captain?"

The Marquess of Drake, a Captain in His Majesty's Army when bloody Boney was wreaking havoc throughout the continent had commanded Lucien in battle. Revered as a war hero, the powerful nobleman glanced up from his ledgers. "Jones," he greeted, his tone gave little indication to his thoughts. He tossed his pen down and motioned him forward.

Lucien wandered deeper into the room.

"Sit," the marquess commanded.

He furrowed his brow. "Sit?" Long ago, he'd become suspicious of summons. Those issued by his family, former friends, and now, his employer.

"That is unless you prefer to stand through our meeting?" the other man asked dryly.

Actually, he did. His years of fighting had taught him the perils of rest. *The bloody war.* At the marquess' questioning look, however, Lucien claimed the closest leather, winged back chair. He surveyed the room a long moment, remembering back to a different office, of equally opulent wealth, a world he'd once belonged to but had shunned after the hell visited upon him by life.

His employer began without preamble. "You are unhappy in your new post."

Lucien stiffened. Lord Drake's words weren't a question but rather a flawless observation from a man whose uncanny insight had saved any number of men on any number of occasions. Lucien had done any number of reprehensible things to survive and would likely burn in hell for those sins and others that still kept him awake at night, but he'd never been a liar. "No," he said gruffly. He missed his station in the stables. Mayhap more than he missed his bloody left arm.

"You don't belong in the stables," the marquess said with a directness Lucien appreciated.

"I don't belong here," he tossed back, honestly. Though in truth, he didn't belong anywhere. He was a man who didn't truly fit in any one world.

The other man placed his elbows on the table and leaned forward. "I suspect you belong here more than anywhere else." He arched an eyebrow.

He stiffened, preferring an existence in which his secrets were his secrets and only he had to suffer the torment of them.

Lord Drake held a hand up. "I wouldn't ask or expect a man to divulge his past. That belongs to you, Jones."

The tension eased from his shoulders.

"There is no one I trust more with the running of my household than you," the marquess continued.

Rigidity crept into his frame and the urge to ask for the restoration of his previous post was a physical one. He spoke bluntly. "The staff is afraid of me." And with good reason. He was a dark, miserable monster who'd forgotten how to be a wholly proper gentleman.

The other man's lips turned up in one corner. It didn't escape Lucien's notice that he didn't disagree. "I'll not keep you in a post you don't want."

That magnanimous gesture gave him pause. "Captain?"

"I am in need of a new steward." He motioned to the opened ledgers before him. "My previous steward has done something of a deplorable job."

Lucien sank back in his seat as with the marquess' words went the last of his hope.

"You don't belong in the stables, Jones," the marquess spoke in the quiet, resolute tones of one who'd formed an opinion and would not renege. His lips twisted in a wry smile. A damned captain until he died, the man would be.

Lucien slid his gaze over to the window and stared out at the annoyingly bright, sun-filled sky. He detested the sun, far preferring the gray, overcast London skies and the frequent bouts of rain that better suited his moods. He scrubbed his remaining hand over his eyes. The last place he cared to be consigned was to the countryside that would serve as a forever reminder of the life, nay the lives, he'd left behind—a wife, a child he'd never met. And yet, this man, the marquess and his wife had pulled him back from the edge of despair, restored him to at least a living, breathing shell of a person he'd once been. And for that, he owed them his allegiance.

"I'll have you decide, Jones, which you prefer," the marquess continued. There was no decision here. "You need but let me know." He inclined his head, in a polite dismissal.

Would the man force him to give up the security he'd known and accept that position of steward? Lucien wanted to believe not, but having fought under the man in battle, knew the marquess' mind had already been set and would not be swayed. For all the control Lucien believed he'd possessed these years, he was proven wrong yet again.

He stood and sketched a stiff bow. "Captain," he said between clenched teeth and then took his leave, taking care to close the door quietly behind him. With space between him and his employer, he fed the annoyance that roiled in his gut. He stomped through the damned house. With the thin carpets lining the corridors and the Chippendale furniture, it may as well have been any other London townhouse. Or worse, one in particular. One he still could not shut from his mind, for all his trying. A place where another man had commanded and Lucien had listened. The past blurred with the present as with the marquess' requests, the hint of English countryside flitted through his mind, nearly gutting him. How markedly different his life would have been if he'd possessed the strength to reject another man's requirements of him, for him.

He stopped and pressed his forehead against the ivory, silk wallpaper lining the hall. He drew in shallow breath after shallow breath, concentrating on the quick intakes of air coming into his lungs and the air going out. The memories of war and his return slipped in, refusing to relinquish their hold. With all the bullets he'd taken at the bloody French's hands and the sabers stuck into his skin, by all rights he should have died.

His wife, Sara had sustained him. The letters she'd written, but more, the memory of her, smiling and serenely beautiful, waiting for his return. But the letters had stopped. He'd crafted all manner of explanations for the sudden absence of those notes. Only his return had proven that which, he'd denied himself. She'd died. He steeled his jaw. She'd died and his bloody family had kept that truth from him.

Lucien thrust back useless, bitter regrets and instead fixed on the irony. He'd survived more pistol balls being shot through his body and bayonets slicing his skin, and his wife should have died—of a fever. Oh, the Devil had a wicked sense of humor. Lucien shoved away from the wall and forcibly thrust the memory of her into the past, where it belonged.

He continued down the hall, carefully schooling his expression, and adopting the firm, unyielding mask he'd donned through the years.

A knock sounded at the front door and he marched toward the responsibility that had given some empty sense of purpose these two years since the marquess had pulled him from London Hospital—and back into the living.

The slight pounding at the front door ceased. And then began again with a renewed enthusiasm. "Bloody hell," he muttered. He'd spent so many years away from the life of nobility, he'd forgotten that patent sense of arrogance. The doors opened at will by people whose sole purpose in life was to serve their pampered needs. With each step, with each knock, the fury burned inside. He fed it, because it momentarily quashed the memory of Sara and his great loss.

Another damned knock. Gritting his teeth, he continued striding forward. Whoever the hell was here to see the marquess or marchioness had about as much patience as Boney's forces had in their march through Russia. Suddenly, finding an almost delight in the impatience of the damned noble on the other side of that door, he slowed his steps.

Eloise paused, frowning at the angry, lion knocker on the center of the black door. She fished around her reticule and pulled out the note she'd all but committed to memory when it arrived last evening.

> *My Dear Lady Eloise,*
> *I do so hope you'll join me for tea…*

"At one o'clock," she murmured aloud, stuffing the note into her reticule. She dimly registered the interested stares directed her way by the lords and ladies passing by at the fashionable hour.

Humph. She turned and peered out into the street. Perhaps the marchioness had meant a different day at one o'clock? But no, no, that wouldn't make sense. Her driver remained patiently at the edge of the street, a pained expression upon his face at his mistress' bold display. Eloise bristled with indignation. She couldn't very well leave. And furthermore, mayhap the real area of concern lay not, in fact, with her public showing of eagerness at the marchioness' doorstep, but rather the absence of a likely, indolent butler.

She knocked again. Whoever would imagine that the powerful, respected, and oft revered Marquess and Marchioness of Drake should have such inattentive servants? Eloise screwed her mouth up tightly, realizing even as the thought slipped into her musings how wholly arrogant it must seem.

Especially one who was merely a knight's daughter. Another knock. *Who is hardly sought after at the leading* ton *events.* Another knock. Not that she cared either way about leading *ton* events. A strand of blonde hair escaped her serviceable chignon and fell over her eye. She tucked it behind her ear and, with a sigh, at last conceded that her serendipitous meeting with Lady Drake and the fateful offering of tea had merely been too much good fortune for one who was slated with nothing but bad luck. With a sigh, Eloise turned around.

The click of the door opening met her ears just as the tips of her right foot touched the step down.

"May I help you?"

That harsh, gravelly voice froze her in her steps. Perhaps her fortune was not all bad, after all. Heart thumping wildly in her chest, Eloise spun around. Emotion swelled in her breast at the first sight of him, after all these years. She searched for glimpses of the young man he'd been, but saw none in the harsh set to his mouth and hard stare. Well over a foot taller than her mere five feet two inches, she moved her gaze up the towering butler with a crop of thick, black hair. Ruggedly beautiful with sharp, angular cheeks and a chiseled nose slightly curved from a punch he'd been dealt by an angry Richard. Her gaze lingered upon the empty place his arm had once been, the jacket neatly pinned up. Pain pierced her heart and she tamped down all pity. He'd neither welcome nor did he deserve that useless sentiment.

"May I help you?" Lucien repeated, with a snappish tone that brought her shoulders back.

The nerve of him. Eloise met his gaze squarely and then froze, her mouth dry. Their lives may be inextricably intertwined yet his piercing gray stare, the same that had haunted both her dreams and nightmares, belonged to a stranger. And the agony of missing him, the joy of being reunited with him all blended, robbing her of thoughts, speech, and movement. Eloise touched trembling fingers to her lips.

Lucien ran a punishing gaze up and down her person. A chill stole through her. She reassured herself he'd merely failed to recognize the friend of his past. She registered the flicker of awareness in his intelligent eyes and she detested that this beautiful reunion should come on the front steps of a stranger's townhouse for all the passing, bored peers to see. "Eloise?"

She managed a jerky nod. Happiness swelled in her breast. "Lucien." Oh, how she'd missed him.

"What the hell are you doing here?" he growled with none of the warmth and gentleness she'd always known from him.

Eloise stared unblinkingly at Lucien. Surely she'd heard him—

"By God, I said what the hell are you doing here?" He yanked her by the arm and jerked her through the front doors.

Oh, dear. She swallowed hard. She'd had years to prepare for this very moment and yet remained as she invariably was—without words. "Oh, Lucien," she said, her voice hoarse with emotion. Lucien released her arm with such alacrity she stumbled. "It is so wonderful to see you." She had missed him more than any person in her life. God help her, even the husband who'd been kind and good to her still had never managed to evoke the emotion inspired by Lucien Jones. Suddenly, the joy of seeing him erased the years of propriety drilled into her in her role as countess. She flung her arms about him.

He grunted and staggered under the unexpectedness of her embrace. His broad, powerful frame was more muscular than she remembered. She mourned the loss of that one arm, and hurt with a need to have him wrap it about her as he'd done so many times when she'd been a small girl, so hopelessly in love with him. Tears flooded Eloise's eyes and she blinked them away, not wanting him to see them and interpret them as signs of pity.

With his remaining arm and the strength of his chest, he set her away. "What in hell are you doing, Eloise?" he hissed.

She cocked her head. "Lucien," she began. "It is me," she said lamely. Obviously, he could see that it was, in fact, Miss Eloise Gage. Granted, she was not the same plump child he likely remembered on the eve of having her first London Season. Her blonde, impossibly tightly curled tresses were the same as was the lone birthmark at the corner of her lip. He used to tease her mercilessly about it. Surely, he even now recalled the blasted mark?

As though following her unspoken thoughts, his gaze shifted lower, ever lower, and fixed upon that slight mark. A smile played about her lips. Then his mouth set in a hard, unmoving line. At the left corner of his eye, a muscle ticked, hinting at his annoyance. She shook her head, uncomprehending this aloof stranger. She tried again. "Lucien—"

"Do not call me by my name, madam." That sharp command better suited to the battlefield than a formal foyer, came out as an angry whisper. He shot a furious glance about for interlopers.

All her earlier joy was replaced by confusion, then hurt, and ultimately gave way to a seething annoyance. She snapped her eyebrows into a single line. "What should I call you?"

"You, madam, are not to call me anything."

Eloise recoiled. "What are you on about?" His coolly aloof tone was more painful than had he slapped her.

It was as though her words didn't penetrate whatever walls he'd constructed about himself these years. With quick, clipped steps, he proceeded to pace the rich, Italian marble floor. "How did you discover my whereabouts?"

A pang struck her heart. "You didn't want to be found?" Did that ghost-like whisper belong to her? But the pain of that possibility...oh, God, all these years she'd thought of him, and ultimately, he'd not wanted to be found. She pressed her eyes tightly closed as his gleaming, black boots beat a staccato rhythm upon the floor. For years she'd believed he'd removed himself from her life in an effort to avoid his father. Theirs had been a volatile relationship that had been forever damaged when the viscount insisted his son take a commission in the military, instead of the church as Lucien had wished. But this, now knowing..."You avoided me." All these years she'd ached for him... missed his friendship...*their* friendship. And she'd mattered not at all.

He ignored her question. "Does my father know I'm here?"

She flattened her lips into a firm line.

Lucien spun back and took her shoulder in his hand. "Does he—?"

17

"N-no," she stammered and for the first time terror filled her at the presence of this dark, angry stranger.

Some of the tension left him.

Perhaps this was about nothing more than the feud from long ago between the Viscount Hereford and his third son. Eloise held her palms up. "He doesn't know you're here," she softly assured him. She curled her toes tightly with guilt. If this cold, unyielding man before her learned she'd searched for him all so she might try and bring peace to his fractured family, he would have tossed her quite handily out onto the front steps, rules of propriety and friendship between them be damned.

Lucien lowered his head and she drew back from the ice glinting in his thunderous gray stare. "Then. What. Do. You. Want?" he asked on a lethal whisper.

"I—" She wet her lips.

He followed that movement and for a desperate moment she imagined he might kiss her, which was, of course, silly because Lucien had never desired her. He'd loved her. Cared for...but Sara had held his heart. Eloise had merely held his friendship.

His lips pulled back in a menacing sneer. "I asked, what—?"

Only, now it appeared she'd never even held that.

"Lady Sherborne!" Their gazes flew as one to the Marchioness of Drake. She came down the stairs, the ease of her smiling visage indicated she'd not detected the thick undercurrents of tension between them.

"Please, Eloise," she insisted, hungering to steal one more glance at the man she'd ached to see these many years.

Lady Drake stopped before them. "Oh, how splendid! I've been waiting for your visit, Eloise."

She had as well. Eloise gulped.

Until this moment.

THREE

Eloise.

L ucien drew back, unsettled, feeling like the unwitting actor upon a stage and he was the only one unknowing of his lines.

Eloise.

Only, this slender, gently curved lady with a trim waist and flared hips, bore no trace of the child he'd played with through the pastures of Kent. As though unnerved by his scrutiny, she lowered her gaze to the marble floor. No, the Eloise he remembered had never done anything as demure as lower her eyes. And she'd been a Miss Eloise Gage, a friend…Had he ever truly had friends?

The stricken expression in her eyes indicated that this older, more mature lady with those very familiar tight blonde curls was very much…. Eloise. She stared boldly at him. Her piercing blue-green gaze ran up and down his frame. Fury and hurt danced in those depths. Then, Eloise had worn her every emotion as plain as if they'd been stamped in ink across the delicate lines of her face.

He fisted his hand, balling it tightly, resenting her insolence in coming here. In reentering this new life he'd carved out for himself, in a world away from the ugly one he'd left behind.

"Jones?"

Lucien jerked. The marchioness' concerned tone cut across the shocking reappearance of his past into his dark future. He gave his head a hard shake. "My lady," he said gruffly.

"We'll be taking tea in the Pink Parlor. Would you see to refreshments?" With that, she looped her arm through Eloise's and ushered

19

the slender young lady onward, their slippers noiseless upon the marble floors. He stared after them until they disappeared into the parlor.

Lucien scrubbed a hand over his eyes, the empty arm socket, cut off at the elbow itched with the memory of movement as he longed to scrub both hands over his eyes and then dig his fingers into his temples until he drove back the dream, hell, or reality this happened to be. Perhaps it was all three rolled into one.

She was here.

What was she doing here?

He lowered his arm to his side and frowned. And who the hell had she wed? Lady Sherborne. Before his father had purchased his damned commission for the infantry, Lucien hadn't spent much time in London. He'd been so thoroughly bewitched, mind, body and soul by the mild-mannered, serenely beautiful Sara to have ever dashed off to take part in the *ton's* inane amusements. And as the third son, he'd been afforded certain luxuries, such as remaining in the country, while his elder brother, the heir to the Viscount Hereford had been expected to dance attendance at *ton* events.

His lip peeled back in an involuntary sneer. Certain luxuries. What a bloody joke. And with Eloise's reentrance into his life, she'd ushered in all the darkest memories he'd sought to bury. His aspirations for himself. His father's goals for him. And the damned viscount's ultimate triumph. May the blighter rot in hell.

Lucien closed his eyes and drew in several slow, steadying breaths; a calming mechanism he'd adopted over the years when the memories became particularly hard to bear. He dug deep and sought purchase within himself to climb from the pit and back to his present.

Eloise. Lady Sherborne.

The Marchioness of Drake.

Refreshments.

Tea, yes, they required tea.

With wooden steps he strode through the house, focused on the task set out. Refreshments were easy. An ugly, mirthless chuckle worked its way up his throat. Mayhap not easy, *per se,* with one and a half arms, but something he now accomplished with enough ease to not rely on others for the simple chore.

He marched down the corridor to the kitchens. The kitchen staff looked to him. "Refreshments," he barked, his voice still gruff from ill-use.

A handful of servants hurried to ready a tray for the marchioness and her guest. Guest. Aye, it was far easier to think of the lady with wounded eyes as a mere guest and not the girl who'd fished and swam alongside him and his brother, Richard, in the Kent countryside. To remember her as she'd been, forced him to think of the day he'd accepted that damned commission, capitulating to his father's urgings, leaving his wife, and stepping into the European theatre masterminded by the power-hungry Boney.

A servant rushed toward the door with the tray.

"I'll see to it myself," he snapped.

The dozen or so of the kitchen staff stared at him, wide-eyed.

She hesitated and then handed it over.

They'd learned early on not to question his abilities or capabilities. He easily handled the silver tray in his steady, stable, strong, right arm and the partial left. With sure footsteps, he made his way to the door. A servant discreetly held it open and he exited the kitchens. With each step that carried him closer to Eloise, he steeled his heart, not allowing himself to think about what brought her here.

He remembered the troublesome minx she'd been as a child enough to know this was no serendipitous meeting with the marchioness. Instead, he chose to focus on this unfamiliar stranger who'd replaced the oft blushing, usually tongue-tied Eloise Gage.

She'd wed a nobleman. A Lord Sherborne. He hoped the blighter was possessed of a tolerant, patient spirit. The Eloise Lucien had long known had the frequent tendency to find herself in all manner of difficulties. He strode down the corridor. And by God he did not intend to allow himself to be her latest manner of difficulty.

He paused outside the open parlor door. A quiet, husky laugh, familiar and all the more aching for that familiarity, washed over him. He clenched his eyes tightly not wanting it to matter that Eloise laughed the way she had as girl and…His mind raced. She must be twenty-seven, nay. She had a birthday two months past, the twenty-fourth of January. She would be twenty-eight now.

And he hated that he remembered that piece of her because it meant he was not as indifferent to Eloise as he cared to believe.

"…I'm so sorry," Lady Drake said softly.

His ears pricked up.

"It is…" The remainder of Eloise's words escaped him.

God help him. If any of the staff spied the butler, the most distin-guished member of the household staff, hovering at the door, eaves-dropping like a chit just from the schoolroom, the marquess would likely sack him with good reason. But for that, he remained rooted to the spot.

"…I cannot imagine the loss…"

His gut clenched. What loss? And for the first time since he'd abandoned the more respectable, honored position as third son to a viscount, he damned the class division that obscured the truth and the remainder of that thought. What had happened to Eloise? After he'd returned and discovered the death of his wife, and a child he'd only learned of on the pages of letters handed him on the battlefield, he'd retreated to London, half-dead, emaciated like a stray dog in the streets, content to die. He'd not thought of Eloise. Or…

The tray rattled in his arm. He silently cursed as the silver clattered noisily. The ladies fell silent. A dull flush climbing up his neck, Lucien stepped inside the room. "My lady," he said, his tone harsh.

Except, his employer, the benevolent Lady Emmaline Drake, had known him when he'd first found a place in London Hospital. She'd sat by his side reading to him, ignoring his surliness and had remained devoted. As a result, she gave no outward appearance of being both-ered by his coarse tone and rough, soldier's speech.

The marchioness smiled. "Thank you, Jones. If you'll set it over here."

"Jones?"

Lucien cursed and nearly upended the tray under Eloise's per-plexed question.

SEDUCED BY A LADY'S HEART

Lady Drake motioned in his general direction. "Jones, my…"

Eloise opened her mouth, likely to correct the marchioness' error. He glowered her into silence and the words withered and died on her lips. She frowned, though the slight narrowing of her eyes indicated she had little intention of allowing the matter to rest.

He continued to glare at her. He had little intention of allowing the stubborn young lady an opportunity to ask her questions, in front of his employer no less. "Is there anything else I may get you, my lady?"

His mistress inclined her head. "No, that will be all."

With a grateful silent exhalation of air, he started for the door, when Eloise's words to Lady Drake froze him mid-step.

"I do not suppose *Jones,*" Lucien growled, his unblinking gaze on the bloody wall in the hall. *Do not say it,* "mentioned we were acquainted as children." Of course, he should have known Eloise enough to know she'd never be reticent merely because he willed it. He shot a glance over his shoulder. Eloise angled her chin up. Her words were directed to the marchioness, her stare trained on him. "We were quite the best of friends."

They had been. In this, the lady spoke the truth. As a young boy he'd not really seen the usefulness in girls. Father had demanded he and Richard entertain his friend's lonely daughter, Eloise. Belligerent as any lad of seven would have been with those directives, it had taken little time for Lucien to find she was unlike any girl he'd ever known. She'd loved to spit, fish, and bait her own hooks. She'd been bloody perfect to a lad of seven.

Lady Drake looked wide-eyed between them. "Indeed?" A pleased smile lit her brown eyes. She motioned him forward. "Jones, you mustn't rush off! However did you not mention such a thing?"

"Oh, I'm sure because he is so very dedicated to his services that he'd never do something as improper as to rekindle an old friendship if it were to in anyway compromise his obligations to your household, my lady." He'd have to be as deaf as a dowager to fail to hear the stinging rebuke in her words.

He hesitated, eyeing the door with the same longing a man with an addiction to drink surely felt for a tumbler of whiskey.

"Don't you dare leave," Lady Drake admonished, a smile in her gentle command.

Lucien turned fully around. He fixed a black scowl on Eloise with a look that would have withered much taller, stronger men. She angled her chin up another notch.

"It has been so long, Emmaline." She lowered her voice to an almost conspiratorial whisper. "Do you know, I believe for a moment Mr. Jonas...*Jones* didn't remember me?" A forced laugh bubbled past her lips.

He frowned. When had Eloise learned the art of false laughter and brittle smiles? As much as he detested her reappearance in his life, he hated even more that innocent, grinning Eloise with that intriguing birthmark at the corner of her lip had been hardened by life. "I should return to my obligations, my lady," he said. He'd never been one to plead. But from the time the surgeon had made the decision to chop off the lower portion of his left arm, he'd not begged anyone for anything. Mayhap if he'd begged his father, begged for that position with the church instead of a damned commission, Sara would now live. In this moment he wanted to beg off, leave the two ladies here.

"Oh, you simply mustn't, Jones!" The faintest command underlined the marchioness' words and he silently cursed, knowing all hope of escape had been effectively ended by the bits of his past Eloise had dangled before his employer.

Eloise averted her eyes, unwilling to meet his gaze. Good, the lady should be bloody terrified. She didn't play with the same lad who'd raced across the hills of Kent. No, Eloise didn't know the man he'd become. She only remembered the man she thought she knew. The one who'd laughed and smiled and loved.

He shifted on his feet, too aware of the station difference between him and these ladies. And he hated that Eloise had reminded him he'd not always been a servant. For there was nothing disrespectful in honest, hard work. Of course, the viscount would never see it that way. He smiled. Oh, that would be the ultimate revenge upon his vile sire. "I have household business to attend to, my lady," he tried again. It was the closest he'd come to begging.

Something reflected in Lady Drake's eyes. Possessed of a kinder heart than most of the empty-headed, vain members of the *ton*, she saw more. She must have seen something in his expression for she inclined her head and the laughter dimmed in her eyes. "Of course, Jones."

He sketched a bow and, without a backward glance for Eloise, all but sprinted from the room, feeling the same freeing sense of relief he'd felt when he'd fled Kent after learning of Sara's death.

FOUR

Eloise tried to smile. She tried to drum up suitable repartee and dialogue for the kind, warmhearted marchioness who'd been so gracious to invite her to visit when no one in Society really invited Eloise anywhere.

She tried. She really did. But failed miserably. Quite miserably. Eloise accepted the proffered cup of tea, grateful for something to hold in her slightly trembling fingers. She raised the glass of tepid brew to her lips and sipped, all the while aware of the marchioness' curious stare trained upon her. She took another sip.

"I hope you know," the marchioness began and Eloise froze, the rim of her delicate, porcelain glass pressed to her lips. "I would never dare press you for details that I don't have a right to."

The muscles of her throat worked spasmodically. She managed a nod but feared if she spoke her gratitude the other woman would detect the tremor in her words.

Emmaline held up the tray of pastries. "I have a shameful weakness for cherry tarts."

Eloise clung to the offered change of discourse and set her tea-cup down. "Then who doesn't?" She plucked one of the confectionary treats from the tray and the other woman laid the small platter upon the marble top table.

They shared a smile and sat in companionable silence for a long while, nibbling at their respective pastries.

The marchioness was the first to break the silence. "Ours was not necessarily a chance meeting, was it?" There was no rebuke, no outraged shock in that question, sentiments the woman was entitled to.

The dessert crumbled to ash in Eloise's suddenly too-dry mouth. She choked around the bite and picked up her cup once more. She took a sip.

Emmaline waited patiently. Then, according to what she'd learned of the woman who'd been betrothed as a child and waited nearly twenty years for her intended, the returned war hero Lord Drake, to come up to scratch—she was quite adept at waiting.

Eloise sighed, humbled not for the first time. "No," she admitted, shamed by the woman's discovery. "I'm sorry." How very inadequate that apology was for this woman who'd been nothing but kind, when most members of the *ton* were usually nothing but coolly polite to Eloise. She flicked her gaze over to the entrance of the room, but, of course, he would not be there. Lucien had responsibilities, of which she'd never been one. At the pain of that, she tightened her fingers around her glass.

As though sensing her disquiet, Emmaline laid her fingers upon Eloise's hand and she lightened her hold upon the fragile cup. "You needn't apologize," she assured her. "Truly." She winked. "I imagine you've not coordinated a meeting with me based on nefarious purposes."

"Oh, no, indeed not. I....oh…" Heat splashed her cheeks at the teasing glimmer in Emmaline's eyes. "You are teasing."

"Yes." The other woman sat back in her seat. "As you're likely aware, there are not enough opportunities for a good teasing."

"Oh, I'm aware," she muttered under her breath. The moment she'd entered the glittering world of polite Society, she'd come to appreciate how staid, stiff, and generally unpleasant members of the peerage were, and most especially to young women like Eloise, who did not boast the most distinguished of familial connections.

"Forgive me," the marchioness murmured. "I'd pledged to not press you for answers and yet, here I am doing that very thing."

Eloise shook her head. "No, you aren't." She wrinkled her nose. Or perhaps the woman had inadvertently sought answers to questions of the man named Lucien Jonas, or as she knew him, Jones. "I didn't feel you were," she added, reassuringly.

All the while she wondered with a dry humor what the pompous, always proper Viscount Hereford would say to the knowledge his son had altered his surname. That would likely be the final nail in the failing viscount's steady decline.

Which only reminded Eloise of the desperate search she'd launched for Lucien and the discovery that had led her to London Hospital. She stared down at her palms, transfixed by the crescent scar on the inner portion of the wrist, remembering the day she'd received that particular mark. Reluctantly, she raised her head. "You are correct. I…" Her cheeks burned with embarrassment. "I sought you out under information I'd gleaned from a servant in your employ." She winced. Proud, powerful, noble Lucien had forsaken the life of comfort he'd known and, by the fury in his eyes at her reentry into his life, embraced this new life.

Emmaline held a hand up. "You needn't say anything more," she said quietly.

She braced for the stiff disapproval…that did not come.

The marchioness trailed a distracted finger halfway around the rim of her cup and then back again. She repeated the movement several times, her gaze directed inward. Then she paused, her index finger on the center of the rim. "Do you know how I met Mr. Jones?"

Her heart stuttered. "I do not," she said between tense lips, both craving a piece of the missing years of his young life and fearing the words the woman might impart. The crisp, clean, yet lonely, London Hospital flashed behind her eyes. The broken, sorrowful men in their beds. The muscles in her stomach tightened with thoughts of Lucien as alone and somber as the Lieutenant-Captain.

"He was a patient at London Hospital," Emmaline finally said.

She battled a momentary twinge of regret at the already known fact. Eloise cleared her throat and glanced guiltily over at the door, detesting gossip, but this was different. Wasn't it? She turned her attention to the marchioness. "What was he like?" her voice emerged a hoarse croak. Please, say he was one of the charming, smiling sort like the soldier Emmaline had read to earlier yesterday afternoon.

A sad light lit the woman's pretty, brown eyes and the knot in Eloise's belly grew. "He was…serious. Quiet."

Her heart spasmed. Of course he had been. He'd returned from war to discover his wife and his son, a child he'd never even met, dead and gone. Eloise clenched her eyes tightly. Would he blame her if he knew the truth? Would he see she'd failed Sara and Matthew and, in doing so, failed him? How could he not?

"I do not know if you are aware of the losses he suff—"

"I am aware," she said, her voice rough with emotion. Eloise coughed into her hand. "Forgive me for interrupting."

Emmaline cocked her head and studied her. At the marchioness' scrutiny, Eloise shifted in her seat. Only as the long-case clock ticked away the passage of silent moments, the resolve that had driven her these past six months stirred to life with a renewed vigor. She'd known when she ultimately found Lucien and presented the truth of his father's circumstances, he'd likely flatly reject her request to return to Kent, to his family's fold. Yet, she'd believed with every fiber of her being she could ultimately convince Lucien to see his father and brothers and again know a semblance of the peace—a peace they'd had before life had shown them the cruelties of existence.

It was that resolve that allowed her to raise her head and meet Emmaline's patient stare. "It is not my place to discuss the circumstances of Lucien…" She warmed. "Mr. Jona…*Jones*', past. However, I have news of his family." News he'd rather likely never care about hearing. "And I would not forgive myself if I somehow failed to bring him and his family together." She knew that because she'd suffered too many losses where words had gone unfinished, pledges incomplete. Lucien might not believe he would ever move in a world with anything but anger and resentment for the father, who'd secured his commission, but the time would come…and he deserved that closure.

Emmaline touched her palm to her mouth. "Oh, my," she said softly.

Yes, the loss of her husband had shown Eloise that there were never adequate words to capture an appropriate level of sympathy for death and impending death. Eloise longed to share the burden she'd carried these many years, but had been alone for so long, she oft forgot how to speak freely, and unfortunately with marriage to Colin, she'd been thrust into a society that did not value or welcome those honest, unfiltered words.

So, the secrets she'd carried, the same ones that haunted her dreams and days, remained firmly buried beneath the surface seen by none, suffered only by her.

"Whatever you or..." Emmaline looked to the door. "Mr. Jones may require, you need but ask."

It was a gracious, sincere offer from an equally sincere woman. "Thank you," she said. Though she could not impose upon the woman's kindness more than she'd already done. Any other noblewoman would have had her tossed out for her clear orchestration of a meeting with their lead servant. Eloise finished her tea and set the cup down on the table. She came to her feet.

Emmaline immediately followed suit. "You must promise to visit again." A mischievous sparkle reflected in her eyes.

Eloise widened her eyes with a sudden understanding. And for a moment, the two practically strangers, forged a bond as two ladies who according to what she'd gleaned from the gossip columns, both had known a similar unrequited regard. She gave a slight nod. "Thank you." She paused. "For everything."

Emmaline inclined her head and with a final smile, Eloise started for the door and then froze. She spun back around.

A question reflected in Emmaline's eyes.

"It...I...my visit to the hospital, it was not solely about..." She flushed. "Arranging a meeting with you." She'd needed to see the place Lucien had called home for too long. She'd needed to know about his life after war and Sara and Matthew. And she'd hated the glimpse she'd had into his world. All those words went unspoken.

"I know," Emmaline said simply. She crossed over and rang the bell. "I could tell that with a single glance of you at London Hospital."

Eloise wrinkled her brow. "How—?" The words on her lips died as Lucien appeared.

Emmaline smiled. "Jones, will you please escort Lady Sherborne out." She held Eloise's gaze. "Again, I look forward to your continued visit."

FIVE

He always possessed powerful, long legs. Unfairly long, she'd always said as a girl. He'd always raced faster than her, an unfair advantage made all the greater by the skirts she'd donned as a small girl.

Eloise grit her teeth, quickening her steps to keep up with the deuced pace he'd set for them. He stalked purposefully through the enormous townhouse. She drew to a stop and waited for him to note her absence.

He turned right at the end of the corridor.

Filled with annoyance at his high-handedness, she tapped the tip of her slipper on the thin, red carpet and folded her arms across her chest.

Lucien came back around the corner, a thunderous expression on his face.

At the menacing stare trained on her, a desire to flee this fierce, scowling stranger consumed her. Eloise dug her toes into the carpet, refusing to be cowed. This was Lucien. He continued, coming closer. The boy who'd taught her to bait her hooks and fly fish. Gone were all traces of the grinning person he'd been.

He stopped with five feet of space between them. "My lady," he bit out.

Eloise searched for Lady Emmaline before realizing..."Are you referring to me?" she snapped.

"What else would you have me call you, my lady?" She flinched at the coarse, clipped tones of his speech. Gone were the smooth, polished tones perfected by a nobleman's son. "What?" he taunted. "Do you wonder what has happened to the fine gentleman you remember?"

"Yes," she said with a bluntness that momentarily froze him. She quirked an eyebrow. "Come, now? Surely you'd not believe I would not note this transformation in you." A transformation she didn't like but certainly understood. When life robbed you of innocence and introduced you to ugliness, you either retreated into yourself, or allowed it to destroy you. She'd retreated. Eloise passed a sad glance up and down his beloved frame. Lucien had been destroyed.

She shook free the chill of that thought. No, she had to believe there was still…

"I see the look in your eyes," he spat. "I know what you are thinking."

"Do you?" she tossed back, not knowing where she found the courage to hurl a rejoinder at his harshly beautiful face.

"You wonder what happened to me." He continued as though she'd not spoken. "You see the boy of your youth. A viscount's son."

She sucked in a breath. "That isn't fair," the child's words tumbled from her lips, unheeded, unchecked. "I never cared about that, Lucien," she said wounded by this charge. "It never mattered to me if you were…"

"A nobleman or a servant," he said, his lips curled up in a jeering smile.

Ah, he saw her as a lady now. One who surely valued her new station and likely spurned the life he'd crafted as a servant. Then, he'd been gone many years now. He did not know she'd entered into a glittering world to which she'd never, nor would ever, truly belong. Wedding an earl didn't make a young lady who'd not left the countryside until her eighteenth year a lady or hostess. It merely made her a countess. Eloise took a step. "Do you imagine I would judge you for being a servant?"

His body stiffened at her question.

She advanced toward him. Did he, too, have a desire to flee? Yet, the man she knew him to be possessed too much courage to leave. Eloise stopped with a mere hairsbreadth between them. She tilted her head back and looked up his impossibly tall, powerful form. "I was never that woman, Lucien. You may now spurn my presence here, but you know that. And you may be mean and angry and hurt, but you are no liar." They stood so close she detected the slight, nearly imperceptible narrowing of his steel gray eyes.

Had he always been this blasted terrifying? She swallowed hard and when he remained silent, she asked, "Did I say mean?"

"You did." The ghost of a smile played on his firm, sculpted lips.

Or did she merely imagine the slight grin there? She tipped her chin up. "Because you are. *Mean.*" Hurling that ineffectual charge at him did not eliminate any of the unease around this new, harder version of the young man she remembered.

"And angry," he pointed out.

It didn't escape her notice that he'd omitted the very key word of hurt.

"It seemed worth mentioning twice," she said, her voice breathless with an awareness of him.

His chest moved up and down in deep, rapid breaths and he slowly dropped his gaze to her mouth. Some emotion flashed in his eyes. Her heart pounded wildly. *He desires me.* Or were those merely her own yearnings? Then, Lucien moved his eyes lower and he settled his stare upon her décolletage. She closed her eyes a moment. There was a place reserved in hell for her, because in this instance, she didn't care that his heart had died with Sara. She wanted him and she would never forgive herself if she moved through the remainder of her lonely existence never knowing the taste of him.

Eloise leaned up on tiptoe.

His body jerked erect. "What are you—?"

She brushed her lips against his. She kissed him as she'd longed to for too many years and then with the dream she'd always carried, his lips reluctantly met hers in a hesitant meeting.

Yet he did not pull away. Emboldened, Eloise twined her arms about his neck, twisting her fingers in the thick, black strands of his silken, soft hair. "Lucien," she whispered against his lips. *I have missed you.* Only, if she breathed those words into existence, he would pull away.

Lucien stiffened at her use of his name and then he folded his arm about her, drawing her close. He slanted his lips over hers again and again. Gone was the hint of warmth, instead replaced with this blaze of fire. He plundered her mouth with his and she welcomed the swift, hot invasion as she met his bold thrust and parry with one of her own.

He drew back and Eloise moaned her regret, but he merely trailed his lips down the side of her cheek. "Lucien," she pleaded. Her words may as well have had the same effect as a bayonet piercing his skin.

He pulled his arm away and retreated…one step…two…and three, eyeing her like she was a two-headed serpent come to destroy. "What are you doing here?" he asked now in total for a third time.

The truth hovered on her lips—the pledge she'd made to his brother, Richard. No, that wasn't truthful. If she couldn't be honest with him, at least she could manage honesty to herself. *I love you.* "I—"

"You found a titled lord, did you, Ellie?" he asked, using her girlhood moniker, though it wasn't as warm or teasing as it once had been. "What would Lord Sherborne say to his wife kissing the Marquess and Marchioness of Drake's servant?" His words, cruel and mocking, lashed against her heart.

Eloise fisted the fabric of her gown. "My husband is dead," she managed.

Lucien opened his mouth and closed it. He opened his mouth once more. "I didn't know," he said, gruffly, in his stranger's voice. Not the gentle friend she'd once known.

Eloise shrugged, feigning indifference, though she was anything but. Tension hummed through her body with the knowledge of his kiss at long last, if even from this dark, unyielding man. "How would you?" she asked softly. The man he'd been would have taken her in his arms and cradled her close. He would have allowed her to cry and helped drive back, if not completely erased, the guilt that dogged her. "You left." *Me. You left me, as though I was as guilty as your father for that damned commission.*

The man he was now did none of those things. The harsh, angular planes of his face remained set in an inscrutable mask, as though she were a nuisance he'd be glad to rid himself of.

"You shouldn't be here," he said, his voice painfully detached. He slashed his hand through the air. "I've created a life for myself and I'll not go back to the life of indolent gentleman."

She folded her arms across her chest, to ward off the chill of his eyes, not knowing where she found the strength to say, "No, Lucien. *You* shouldn't be here."

He lowered his head, so close his coffee-and-mint breath fanned her face. "Why, because there is no value in the work I do?" She fixed on the one familiar scent, one unfamiliar because it was easier than focusing on the vitriol in his eyes.

Then isn't that what he'd become? Two men combined into a person who was both stranger and a friend of her past?

"I never said that," she said firmly. "I would not pass judgment on you—"

He snorted.

Eloise buried a finger into the hard wall of his chest and he grunted. "Very well, I'll be honest with you if you'll not be honest with me—"

"How have I not been honest—?"

"You've hidden yourself away from me," her cheeks warmed at the veiled look he gave her. "Your family," she hurriedly amended. "Where is the honesty in that?"

His cheeks turned a mottled red at her charge.

Good, he should be ashamed of the way in which he'd shut her out of his world. "And when I do see you, you're nothing more than a snarling, sneering, brutish beast I don't recognize."

"That is who I am," he spat. He'd respond to that, then. Why? Was that the safer question? What had he hidden from?

She shook her head, dislodging a blonde curl. It fell unchecked over her brow. "No. No, it's not." And because she'd somehow dug deep to find the courage to challenge him, she pressed ahead. "You are the Viscount of Hereford's son," she reminded him.

The slight stiffening of his body indicated the volatile tension running through him but damn it, she had waited years to say her piece to him.

"And that matters because he is a noble."

"It matters because he is your father," she returned.

"My father is dead." He spoke in such deadened tones, her body chilled over.

"No, he is not," she said when at last she managed to speak. She bit the inside of her cheek to keep from pointing out that soon he would be. In his fury, that truth likely wouldn't make a difference to Lucien.

Eloise reached for his hands and went still as she belatedly registered the loss of that precious limb. An aching pain pressed on her chest, but she buried those futile regrets. He'd never accept or welcome her sympathies and he deserved more than those useless emotions anyway. "It is time you return to the life you left. Your father, your brothers." *Me.*

A hard, mirthless grin marred his lips, a cruel rendering that said he'd noted her misstep. "You do not approve of my new station, Eloise?"

She took his remaining hand between hers and ignored the nearly imperceptible narrowing of his eyes. "I would never, ever demean the work you do. I think it is admirable." How many gentlemen would forsake the comforts known, even as a third born son, and instead embrace a life of servitude? That was the man of character he'd always been—the man she'd fallen in love with. Eloise turned his palm over, the large, callused hand, a hand that no longer belonged to a gentleman. Different. And yet, the same. The same hand that had caught her as she'd jumped from a fallen birch tree into the lake upon his father's property. The same hand that had plucked the splinters from her fingers when she'd landed in a bush of thorns.

"I don't need your lies or platitudes," he spoke into the quiet and reluctantly she released her hold upon him. Lucien looked back and forth, of course the one who registered the place in which they discussed these intimate matters. He flexed his jaw. "If this is about me," it was, "then do not come back. Let me live now as I would."

They studied each other in silence; him icily aloof, she seeking signs of the past etched on the harsh planes of his face.

She touched his cheek with the tips of her fingers. "You were never indolent. You were…" Kind. Gentle. Loving. All things good. "You were never indolent," she repeated instead, knowing he would only reject her words of regard. She pressed her fingertips against his lips and cut off whatever spiteful reply he'd toss at her. "It is time you come home."

With that she marched down the hall, him trailing silently behind her, strangers once more.

SIX

L ucien stared at the wide, closed double doors Eloise had just departed through. He had relied on his intuition to serve for the four years he'd spent on the Continent. The one time he hadn't used his intuition had seen him with a Frenchie's bayonet in the flesh of his left arm. It was a wound that, ironically, ultimately festered *after* he'd returned from battle. The loss of that arm had taught him the perils of not trusting his instincts.

It was that same intuitiveness that indicated there was more at play in Eloise being here. Now.

Something had brought Eloise into his life, once more.

And if he remembered at all the gap-toothed, grinning child with sun-reddened cheeks and an unfortunate tendency of repeating back anything he and his brother, Richard, had said, he'd be wise to be wary about the woman she'd become.

He gave his head a clearing shake and started down the corridor, the memory of Eloise and her damned, perfect mouth and her bold kiss emblazoned on his mind. His body still thrummed with a hot awareness of the feel of her in his arms. He blamed the surge of desire still coursing through him on the fact that he'd not had a woman since he'd left his wife and gone off to battle.

Lucien entered one of the marquess' parlors. He came to an abrupt halt. Two maids, at work glanced up from their tasks. Annoyed that he'd be prevented even a moment's solitude, Lucien waved them back to their work. The young women hastily averted their gazes, but not before he detected the flash of fear in their eyes. Over the years, he'd been an object of fear, pity, and sympathy. He tightened his mouth and wandered over to the window. Then, people had good right to fear him. Life had transformed him into a foul, sneering beast. There had been only two individuals who seemed unfazed by his presence, the marquess and marchioness. He frowned. No, that was no longer true. Now, there was a third person uncowed by his miserable presence. *Eloise.*

That isn't altogether true, a silent voice jeered. Her olive-hued skin had gone waxen at the sight of him and his empty coat sleeve. Lucien had long ago accepted the physical loss he'd suffered on the battle-field. He'd even learned to live with the frequent nightmares of soldiers being cut down in battle and their agonized cries as they sucked in a last, shuddery breath of life. Yet, with Eloise's sudden, unexpected and unwelcome appearance, he'd mourned the loss of his arm. The slight tremble on her slightly too-full lips had conveyed louder than any words the one loathsome emotion he abhorred more than all others—pity.

He didn't want pity. And he most certainly didn't want it from her.

He growled and the maids jumped in unison. Lucien ignored them and they resumed their daily task.

His resentment at her visit with the marchioness spiraled. How dare she come here and question the honest, respectable life he'd carved out for himself. He'd been one quick, slightly awkward hand movement away from ending his life and then Lady Drake, in her tenacity, had pulled him back from the edge of despair.

The truth of those dark days, he could at last admit. In her stead-fast devotion, Emmaline had roused thoughts of the girl who'd been friend to him and Richard through the years. The marchioness had sustained him to the point he'd not taken his life as he'd wished, but ultimately it had been the memory of Eloise, there with her crooked lower row of teeth and the dimple in her right cheek.

From the windowpane he absently studied the maids' meticulous, practiced movements and then shifted his attention to the street below. A grand, black lacquer carriage not unlike the one Eloise had arrived in rattled by, a loud, rolling reminder of the vast difference between them. As children, those differences hadn't mattered. Somehow, their roles had shifted and he, Mr. Lucien Jonas, son of a viscount, now served tea and held doors open for married ladies.

My husband is dead...

His gut clenched at the whispered admission. Not for the first time since she'd arrived did he feel like an utter bastard who'd kicked the kitchen cat. He'd spent the past five years hating his father, hating life, hating that he'd never known his child, held his wife as she died and selfishly never considered Ellie Gage, who'd been a friend. A faint smile turned his lips. A friend, when that is the last relationship young boys ever sought to forge. His smile withered. She too had known loss, no less great than his own.

"Jones, we've finished."

He started and found the young maids patiently waiting, expressions familiarly blank. He gave a nod. They dipped polite curtsies and scurried from the room.

Lucien took a slow, lonely turn about the empty parlor. With the fresco ceilings and gilt frames, the space was still more lavish than any of his viscount father's holdings.

You shouldn't be here...

Eloise's softly spoken words filtered through his mind and melded with the definitive command issued by the marquess earlier that morning. Their charges and concerns all rolled together until their voices blended as one in a cacophony inside his head. He pressed his fingers against his eye in an attempt to blot out the noise of it.

He didn't belong here, yet he didn't belong in his past.

There was no place for him. There was no station that, after his years of fighting and coarsened manners, he truly belonged.

The marquess had presented him an option: life in London in this post he detested where servants feared him, and worse, he'd have Eloise thrust painfully back into his life. Or the respectable post as steward in the countryside where he'd be forced into remembering the person he'd left behind. He tried to bring her memory up, to draw forth Sara's plump cheeks and lush hair, but the image blurred and shifted as Eloise's face danced behind his eyes. "Damn you, Eloise, what have you done?"

And worse...what had brought her here.

With the bond forged between him, Eloise and his brother when they'd been just children, Lucien suspected just what that something was. Or rather who. The muscles of his stomach clenched involuntarily. For years he'd shut his family out of his life. He'd buried the memory of his brothers, father and Eloise, resolved to never see them again. Yet, here was Eloise. And where Eloise was, surely his brothers and father were to follow. Now, he'd wager the sanity he'd secured in these recent years, that his eldest brother, Palmer, had his hand at play here. He fisted his hand at his side.

A bell rang and he welcomed the blessed diversion provided his employer. Glad to thrust memories of Eloise from his mind, he stalked out of the room and strode down the corridors with determined steps. He entered the same parlor Eloise—nay Lady Sherborne—had entered a short while ago. He froze. The marchioness cradled her child, not quite two, upon her lap.

The agonizing regrets flooded him. Of the child he'd never even known, of the wife who'd carried that child for nine months, while he'd missed the opportunity to see her grow round. He cleared his throat and the marchioness jumped. "Forgive me," he said, sketching a bow. "You called, my lady?"

Lady Emmaline smiled, a generous one that reached her eyes. "Oh, you startled me." She wagged a playful finger in his direction. "You always do that."

With his life having been dependent upon that silence through years of battle, one tended to carry those lessons. "My apologies," he said gruffly. He'd likely carry them to his grave.

She shook her head. "I'm merely teasing you, Jones."

He'd forgotten all those old expressions of teasing and laughter and smiling and didn't imagine he'd ever remember them. He fell quiet.

"No sleep," the small girl, Regan tugged at her mother.

"Yes, sleep," she said in a sweet sing-song tone. She motioned to the nursemaid with flaming red hair who rushed forward. The young woman scooped up the girl and carried her from the room. Lady Drake shifted her attention back to Jones and gone was all hint of earlier teasing. "I understand Lord Drake spoke with you about the post of steward."

He stiffened and remained silent.

"When I met you, you were such a dark, lonely man, Jones."

He clamped his lips tight to keep from pointing out that he was still a dark, lonely man.

"I hated seeing you as you were daily and was ever so glad when the marquess offered you a post on our staff." The marchioness stood and wandered over to a rose-inlaid table behind the pale pink, upholstered sofa. She picked up a leather book upon the otherwise immaculate surface and held it out. "Here," she said with a firm set to her mouth that brooked no room for disobedience. This resolute young woman was the same who'd refused to let him turn himself over to death.

On stiff legs, he moved to accept the volume. He looked down at the title. *A Collection of Coleridge's Works.*

"Do you know what that is?"

"My lady?" he said, his tone harsher than he intended. He knew.

"The day you opened your eyes for the first time in London Hospital that was the book I read to you from." She smiled and said gently, "Take it."

He handed it back over. "I can't." More, he didn't want to. What did he have need of a book of poetry? He wasn't the sonnet-reading gentleman he'd been with Sara any longer.

She held her palms upright. "I insist." The resolute note in her words indicated to reject the offering would be the height of rudeness and for all his protestations, Eloise had been indeed correct earlier when she'd said he'd been raised a gentleman. "For whatever reason," the marchioness went on, "you opened your eyes that day. And if you hadn't, and we'd not spoken, and you'd not learned my husband, Lord Drake, had been your commanding officer, and had he not gone to you and eventually offered you employment, you'd not be here."

She paused and looked at him meaningfully. "And after today," *Eloise.* Her meaning as clear as if she'd uttered the lady's name aloud. "Well, after today, I believe you were supposed to be here." A knowing glint lit her eyes. "For very specific reasons."

Lucien's fingers tightened reflexively about the book until he had a white-knuckled grip upon the volume.

"That will be all," she said softly.

He managed a jerky nod and with volume in hand, he strode from the room, hating that he saw the truth in her words.

SEVEN

E loise stared at the double doors with the same sense of dread she had on her first visit to this very place. *You found the marchioness and now found him. You do not need to be here. Leave.* "Coward," she muttered to herself.

"My lady?"

She jumped at Nurse Maitland's bemused question. Eloise dusted her moistened palms together, giving thanks for the gloves that concealed her humiliating fear—an irrational fear she knew. "Uh, nothing," she said belatedly. "I was merely…" Woolgathering. Seeking courage.

The woman gave her a gentle smile and held the door open. "I…" The nurse looked at her questioningly. "I do not require an additional escort," she assured her. "I imagine you are quite busy."

She hesitated. "I'm certain." Not pausing and allowing the woman to protest, she entered through the doors. Her feet, in serviceable boots, padded quietly upon the floor, a wiser selection after her near mishap with the marchioness nearly a week ago.

The men confined to their beds raised first their eyebrows in shock and then their hands in greeting. Her mouth turned up wryly. Then, they'd probably identified her cowardice upon her first visit and marked her as a bored young lady who didn't intend to return.

Shame needled her that she'd not considered them before she'd entered these lonely walls. Lucien had driven her here. The men here, collectively, had brought her back. She kept her gaze trained on their faces and not those stark, white linens that danced around her memory.

She paused mid-stride as the flash of crisp linen from her past nearly blinded her, until all she saw was white. The white of Sara's cheeks, drained of color from the doctor having bled her for too many days. The white of the linens as she'd lain motionless, empty-eyed, staring at the ceiling overhead. Eloise shot a hand out, seeking purchase and finding it on a convenient pillar.

"Are you all right?"'

She jerked and blinked several times as the concerned question pulled her to the moment. With sanity restored, she nodded slowly and looked about for the owner of those words.

A cheerful soldier with a wide-toothed smile met her eyes. The bright shock of his orange-red hair perfectly suited to one of his high spirits. "I'm..." Her words trailed off as she registered the absence of both limbs. She marveled at Lucien's seeming ease in moving through life missing one of those much-needed arms. That this man should miss two...Sadness knifed through her.

His grin widened. "You're afraid of hospitals."

The momentary twinge of pity fled. "Beg your pardon?"

He jerked his chin about. "I've seen you now both times you've entered. You become all queer."

Her lips twitched in an involuntary smile. "Queer?" she asked, appreciating his candor. Eloise wandered closer and edged forward to the lone chair.

"Ah, if I'd but known that such flowery speech could draw such a lovely lady close, I'd have long ago bandied about such compliments."

She laughed, taking a seat beside him. "Indeed, such talk would be sure to turn any lady's head."

He inclined his head. "Lieutenant MacGregor."

A lieutenant. The same distinct rank attained by Lucien, a position that signified wealth and status to grant such a position. "Lady Eloise, the Countess of Sherborne," she said belatedly.

"I didn't believe you'd return," he said with surprising candidness.

"Oh?" She almost had not.

He lowered his voice and waggled fiery eyebrows. "Some of us even had wagers on it."

She supposed she should be scandalized by such an admission but embraced the honesty. Her humor fled. "I almost didn't," she confessed, oddly freed by that truth. Perhaps it was his sudden, unexpected, stoic calm, or perhaps it was that he was a stranger who didn't know of her past or even her present. "I have a fear of the color white." Even as the words left her mouth, her cheeks blazed. "Not merely the color white, but nurses and doctors..." Though she'd not seen the stern-faced, somber doctors with their grim thoughts and dark pronouncements. "I imagine that seems wholly silly," she said her words running together. "And quite irrational." She allowed her gaze to wander to a point beyond his shoulder to the rows of beds.

"I've learned there is sometimes no accounting for some fears," he said pulling her back. "But I've also learned, more often than not, there are reasons for those fears." He paused. "We all have them, my lady."

Eloise thought of the muscle jumping at the corner of Lucien's eye. "Yes," she agreed. "We do, don't we?" She appreciated his admission when everyone else had only seen in her an unfortunate young widow, but not thought much beyond that loss to know all the collective losses she'd suffered, the ones that all together kept her awake.

"And for that fear, you came back." He shifted his body, angling the empty place his arm used to be and she imagined if he'd still possessed his arms he would have held a hand up to her. Her heart wrenched unwittingly at his loss.

Yes, she had. For what would be the alternative? Dwelling in a lonely world with melancholy reminders of who they'd been before they'd matured into somber, altered people?

The door opened. She looked to the front of the room. Her breath caught at the cherished figure who strode through the doors, commanding in his black attire. With his long, graceful strides, this man bore every hint of the noble birthright he'd been born to.

"That is Lieutenant Jonas," Lieutenant MacGregor said, noting her interest. "Though he prefers to be called Jones," he added more as an afterthought to himself.

She said nothing, instead a voyeur as Lucien paused beside a bed to speak to one of the men.

"...He comes every Sunday," MacGregor was saying.

"Does he?" she asked. Hope slipped into her heart. This was the man he had been. Not cold, not unfeeling, but one who'd been a boy of twelve and shrugged out of his jacket to give it to a girl who'd been pushed into the lake by his older brother.

"I imagine it is his day off. I understand he is a butler to the Marquess of Drake."

Lucien stood conversing with a balding gentleman leaning on crutches. He nodded at something the soldier said, that increasingly familiar hard set to his unsmiling mouth held her transfixed. What would it be like to teach those lips to curve up in that teasing half-grin as they once had? The same muscles, the same lips, and yet, a gesture seeming so impossible with the hardened stranger he'd become.

Even with the space between them she detected his whipcord muscles go taut with awareness, noting her scrutiny and she jerked her attention away from him, back to Lieutenant MacGregor...

Whose gaze was now fixed elsewhere. The young gentleman angled his head in greeting. "Hello," he called out.

She swallowed hard, having little doubt who that greeting was intended for.

Bloody hell.

Bloody hell! What was she doing here?

Lucien moved with determined steps along the white walls he'd called home for too many years. First, she'd infiltrated the Marquess of Drake's townhouse, his place of employment. Now, she'd wheedled her way into this place he visited on the lone day he called his own. He stopped before MacGregor, a debt-ridden baronet's second son, who'd fought alongside him in the Thirty-first Regiment. "MacGregor," he drawled, deliberately fixing his gaze beyond the crown of riotous blonde curls.

"Jones," the man called out with his usual, unexplainable cheer. He'd never understood how the man could smile after all he'd seen and all he'd lost.

"It is good to see you," he said, very deliberately ignoring Eloise, though attuned to the nuances of her body's every movement.

"I must warn you, if you've come to fleece me today in a game of faro, I've lovely company instead."

A becoming blush stained Eloise's cheeks.

"I see that," he said, reveling in the pale pink that flared to a crimson hue. "My lady," he murmured.

Eloise sprang to her feet. Her skirts snapped noisily about her feet. "Luci…" She cast a sideways glance at a curious MacGregor. Her blush deepened. In all the years he'd known her, she'd never been one of those blushing, fainting ladies. She'd possessed an indomitable spirit and boldness. Had the unknown Lord Sherborne wrought that affect? He found he rather hated the dead man for that crime.

Then, he was guilty of far greater crimes than hating a dead man.

MacGregor looked back and forth between them, interest piqued. "You know each other," he said as though he'd solved the mystery of life.

"No."

"Yes."

He arched an eyebrow.

Eloise clasped her hands in front of her. "That is, what I meant to say…" The two men looked at her expectantly. "Is yes," she finished lamely.

The lieutenant sat back in his bed. "Well," he said, with no small trace amount of shock. "I'll leave you to your visit."

This time they spoke in unison. "No!"

Lucien tugged at his lapel disliking the unease she roused in him. He preferred his life well-ordered, rigid, devoid of emotion. Not this uncertain, volatile pull between them whenever they came together. "Uh…"

"I should be going," Eloise said quietly. She dropped a curtsy. "Lieutenant MacGregor." Then, she met Lucien's eyes with the directness he remembered of her. "I wouldn't dare interfere with your visit. Forgive me." Her meaning clear; as a servant he had but one day granted his own. She, an elevated lady—a countess—was permitted those small, but valuable luxuries when she desired.

Wordlessly, he stepped aside so she could skirt by him without brushing. He stared after her as she marched with small, precise steps, with the same proud set to her shoulders as evinced by Joan of Arc, herself.

"You're a bloody fool, Jones," MacGregor snorted.

"I don't know what you're talking about," he muttered, gaze trained on Eloise. One of the soldiers, missing his lower two extremities, said something that called her to a stop. Most ladies would have been horrified to visit this place. Not Eloise. An unwitting smile turned his lips with the memory of the day she'd pointed her eyes to the sky and baited a squeamish Richard's hook.

MacGregor noted his continued scrutiny. "Then you're an even bigger fool than I imagined."

He yanked his attention away from Eloise and frowned. "You don't know anything about it."

"I might not have the use of my arms, but I have perfect use of my eyes and I saw the way that lady studied you."

Lady. And with the great class divide between them, now as unattainable as the Queen of England. "She's a bloody countess," he added. Not that he had any interest of the romantic sort with Eloise Gage, now the Countess of Sherborne. His heart was dead.

So why did the hint of warmth stir the damned organ at the smile on her full lips?

"And you're a nobleman's younger son playing at servant." The man's rejoinder contained a stunning seriousness that stiffened Lucien's spine.

"I know her," he conceded at last.

The lieutenant scoffed. "Impossible," he said, that one word utterance laced heavily with sarcasm.

A mottled flush heated his neck and he resisted the urge to loosen his cravat. "We were friends as children." He shifted under the man's scrutiny, not understanding this compulsion to explain away his relationship with Eloise.

An appreciative glimmer flicked to life in MacGregor's eyes as he looked down the rows of beds to where she still stood talking to the same man. "That woman is a child no more."

Something tightened in his gut at the primitive interest in the other man's eyes. And it was wholly foolish to feel this masculine possessiveness for Eloise. But Goddamn it. "Close your damned mouth," he snapped, knowing he was being a surly bastard. "You're drooling like a stray pup over the lady."

Instead of taking offense, his words restored the man's usual merriment. He tossed his head back and laughed. "And you are not a man who still sees a child in her," he said.

He glanced about to see how far those too-loudly spoken words had traveled. Eloise remained fully engrossed in conversation with the man at her side. Lucien stared unashamedly at the two of them. She needn't remain by the man's side for...he yanked the timepiece given him as a youth by his father many years earlier and consulted it...well, however many minutes. It must have been a good ten or so. Entirely too long and...

She nodded and then continued on her way and walked through those double doors.

He rocked on his heels. Good. She'd taken her leave.

"If it's all the same to you, I'd suggest you go after the lady and spare the rest of us your miserable company and brilliant skillset at faro and whist."

He made a crude gesture that redoubled the man's laughter. "I..."

"Go," MacGregor prodded and kicked him in the leg, nudging him ahead.

Lucien frowned, hesitating.

MacGregor gave him another kick. "Go," he said again, annoyance and amusement underscoring that one word command.

And then, as if of their own volition, his legs began to move and he walked briskly through the room he'd recently entered. He shoved the doors open and stared down the long corridor. He lengthened his strides. She'd always moved quickly for one so small. Then, a child, who'd found friendship in he and Richard, two slightly older, always taller boys she'd been forced to do so in order to keep up.

Eloise turned the corner and made for the foyer.

"Eloise."

She stumbled and spun around, a hand to the modest décolletage of her sea foam dress. "You startled me." Again. The luxuriant fabric drew out the piercing blue-green of her eyes, momentarily holding him spellbound. The beauty of those eyes reached into his soul and robbed him of breath. She tipped her head. "Lucien?"

He heard the question there and continued forward.

He expected her to retreat, but she remained rooted to the spot. "What do you—?"

"Why are you here?"

Four little lines of consternation appeared as Eloise furrowed her brow. "You stopped me," she said slowly as though speaking to a lackwit.

He cursed. "Not *here*, Eloise. In London Hospital, in the marchioness' parlor."

"I'm not in the marchioness' parlor, silly. I can't be two places at—"

"Eloise," he said in a harsh, impatient tone that killed the teasing edge to her words. In that moment he hated himself more than he ever had before, which was saying a good deal considering the crimes he was guilty of. But he'd never been a bully…until she'd reappeared, making him hate himself for altogether new and different reasons. "Forgive me."

She gave a slight nod.

"Why are you here?" he asked once more. "In my life. I know you enough to know these are no mere coincidences."

Eloise captured the flesh of her lower lip between her teeth and troubled it. "No," she said slowly. "They are not." She raised her soulful eyes to his, the color of the purest, unsullied seas a man would gladly lose himself within. He stiffened. Where had the thought come from? "I missed you," she said in quiet tones.

I missed you, too, Ellie. He tried to force the words past numb lips, but God help him, he couldn't. He couldn't give her the words. To do so would make her believe he was capable of emotions that had died too many years ago.

Eloise searched his face with her sad, wide-eyed gaze, as if seeking those words he could not give.

"Is that why you're here?" He dipped his head. Honey and rosewater, clung to her skin. The two seductive, sweetened scents wafted about, filling his senses, intoxicating. She'd used to smell of fresh grass and country air. "Because you missed me?" He found this new, womanly scent of her a potent aphrodisiac.

"I did." Emotion flooded her eyes and he nearly staggered under the weight of it from this woman he'd once loved as a friend. "I missed you every day you were gone," she whispered.

"Did you?"

"Not a single day passed that I did not think of you." Her admission came out, hoarse with emotion.

A twinge of regret struck him, lashed painfully at his chest. He wished he had the words to at least say he'd entertained thoughts of her. Ellie had deserved that from him. She'd been more part of him than a third hand…a now irony considering the loss that had severed one of those extremities.

She touched a bold finger to his chin, forcing his gaze to hers. "I'd not have you lie and say you thought of me," she said with soft rebuke. "I know the moment you fell in love with Sara that your heart, your every thought, always belonged to her." Her gaze fell to his chin. "Your love was so great there was not enough of it to be shared."

The guilt intensified. Eloise Gage had been the most loyal, devoted friend, and yet the day he'd given his heart to Sara Abbott, he'd not spared her a single thought. Shame filled him, bitter like acid on his tongue. "And what of you, did you love your husband?" He'd not imagined himself capable of prayer any longer, but he mustered a single final one to a God he no longer believed in that she'd at least known love.

A wistful smile stole over her face. "Colin was good to me. He was a friend and I do miss him every day." It didn't escape his notice that she didn't mention the word love.

He hoped the now dead earl had appreciated the gift he'd had in loyal, beautiful Ellie, appreciated her when Lucien never properly had. "What happened?" He didn't know where the question came from.

"He suffered an apoplexy," she said. "He was just twenty-nine when he died."

He had no right to delve into her past. He'd lost that right when he'd forsaken their friendship and yet, he needed to know the pieces of a life he'd missed. "And do you have children?" He imagined a small girl with her riotous, blonde curls and mischievous smile.

"No," she said and the dream of that child flickered out like the flame atop a candle. "We never had children." The muscles of her throat worked. "I am so very sorry about Sara and Matthew," she said.

Grief knifed through him. He sucked in a ragged breath and fought to muster the blasé, obligatory response to her expression of regret. "D-did," he coughed into his hand. "Did you ever know him?" She would have been a young lady, out for a London Season. Likely she'd not had time for the babe of a former childhood friend.

"I did," she said shocking him with the admission.

He stared unblinking at the stark, white walls. And the dream of a child he'd never met and the pain of never having held that child, or known that child before his life was too swiftly ended, became real in ways he'd never experienced before.

Tears flooded her eyes. "He had your smile."

He strained to hear her whispered words and they pierced his heart.

"He was a precocious, stubborn baby." A small laugh escaped her and her gaze grew far away with memories he'd have sold his soul three-times over for. "He would cry with annoyance at not being permitted to feed himself when he was still too young to yield a spoon or fork."

Ah God. He squeezed his eyes tight. "Thank you," he said at last when he managed to look at her once again.

"I've not done anything."

The lone memory would sustain him for the remainder of his lonely days. The memory of a boy who'd looked like him and had his smile and temperament. In that, she'd given him everything. And because the longer they stood here, bodies bent familiarly close to each other, the greater the ache built inside him for a craving that terrified him, he said, "You should go."

Eloise managed a jerky nod. But remained exactly where she stood.

He lowered his mouth close to hers. "What are you doing to me?"

Her thick, golden lashes fluttered wildly. "I l—"

Lucien crushed the remainder of those terrifying words on her lips, claiming her mouth under his once more. This meeting of mouths was gentle, searching, a reunion of two people who'd found each other after great tragedy. She moaned and he slipped his tongue inside to explore the warm, contours of her mouth. With a near physical pain, Lucien drew back. He placed a lingering kiss upon her forehead.

She closed her eyes and leaned into that gentle caress. "Come home with me."

Lucien froze. Her entreaty penetrated the spell she'd woven.

Eloise angled away from him. "Your father is ill." With but the mention of the viscount who'd purchased Lucien's commission and sealed his fate, the light she'd somehow rekindled with her words and kiss went out.

He took a jerky step away from her.

"Lucien," she pleaded.

"Is that what this is?" And at last it began to make sense. "You're here because of my brothers and my father."

She started. A guilty heat burned her cheeks. "I'm here because of me," she corrected, the words coming too late. "I am also here because of Palmer and Richard." She paused. "And your father."

Ah, so she'd come at the bequest of his father and brothers. Because they'd likely known he'd rather see any of his kin in hell, but Eloise, sweet Eloise, the woman he'd called friend, he'd likely never turn away. An ugly laugh worked its way up his throat and she took a step away from him. Good, she should be afraid. He met her searching gaze with stony silence.

"Your father is dying," she said softly.

Shock melded with pain and slammed into him with a lifelike force. *Impossible.* The man he called father was an immovable force; strong, fearless, and untouchable. Regardless——. He forcibly thrust aside pained regrets. "The day he forced that commission upon me, my father was dead to me."

Eloise gasped and touched a hand to her heart. "You don't mean that."

A memory flashed to mind. His father, the powerful, indomitable viscount sneaking away from one of his balls and slipping into the nursery. *Papa! You've come to play soldiers?* Grief sliced through Lucien. That devoted and doting man, he'd loved. Hatred and love warred for supremacy within him.

Then that dark day intruded when he'd been presented with that damned commission.

My son is no coward…

His lips curled up. "I do mean that, Eloise." He peered down his nose at her. "Tell my brothers they wasted their efforts. It would take far more than you, Eloise, to manage a happy reunion with my family."

Her entire body jerked. "Who are you?" she whispered, shaking her head as though she'd had a glimpse of a person she didn't much like.

He balled his hand to keep from taking her in his arm and pleading forgiveness. As she took her leave, he stood staring after her. Just then, he quite concurred with Eloise. He didn't much like himself.

EIGHT

Eloise paced her quiet, lonely parlor, ivory velum in her fingers. A fire crackled in the hearth. She hugged her arms to her chest and rubbed back the unseasonable chill of the spring night, hopelessly wrinkling the sheet she'd received earlier that evening.

This afternoon, at London Hospital she'd captured glimpses of the man Lucien Jonas had been. He reminded her of a kicked and injured dog, craving a soothing touch and yet snarling and stalking away when one wandered too close.

She would have to be a simpleton to have failed to realize what he'd intended with his biting words. He wanted to push her away. All because pushing her away was easier than letting her in. That way, he'd not be hurt again. "You bloody, obstinate fool," she muttered.

She could well-understand his resentment, the need to place blame in light of all he'd lost; from his arm, to his wife, and child. But for that, his father had loved him and he'd throw away that familial bond, not only with his father, but his brothers merely because Richard and Palmer bore the same blood as their sire?

Eloise stomped over to the hearth, page in hand. She held it up to the dim light cast by the orange-red fire's glow and re-read the contents.

My dearest Eloise,

    The viscount's condition has worsened. He continues to ask for Lucien, as well as you. Please convey the urgency to my stubborn brother.

Your loyal servant,

Richard

She folded the sheet and laid it upon the mantel. Then catching the pink, Italian marble between her fingers, she rested her head against the cool stone. What a fool she'd been. In all these years, she'd thought the most difficult task would be in finding a man who'd removed himself from the world and shut out all those who'd loved and cared for him—at least the living ones. She'd never imagined convincing him to come back to her, Richard, Palmer, and his father would be a greater task than the whole six-day creation of the universe.

Eloise released a slow breath, loosening the tension in her chest. She'd once been a lonely girl. There had been no siblings for her to play with. Her mother, who'd died when Eloise had been too young to recall, had left a void in her own household. Lucien and Richard's friendship had sustained her. Most of the joy she'd known in her life had come from the viscount's two sons. For the unconventionality of a small girl slipping into the folds of a male-dominated house, devoid of a motherly presence, it was a forged bond that had quite worked—for all of them.

Eloise's father hadn't had to worry of having a forlorn child underfoot. With an absence of female influence, the viscount and his sons had found some comfort in Eloise's presence.

A log shifted in the hearth. Embers popped and hissed. She stared into the eerie red and orange dancing flames. It was an arrangement that had worked. Or it had, until Sara had entered the village, lovely and all things graceful, and Eloise had ceased to exist. At least for the one man who'd ever mattered to her anyway. Her friendship with Richard had continued through the years. His brother, Palmer, was too busy seeing to whatever heir-like responsibilities one set to inherit had to see to.

She loved them all. But Lucien was the one who'd held her heart. From the moment they'd lain upon their backs and tumbled sideways, giggling and laughing all the way down the sides of the steep hills of Kent only to lay breathless and dizzy staring up at the shifting clouds overhead, her heart had been his.

What do you see, Lucien?

He'd peered up at the vivid, blue skies so long she thought he'd not heard.

I see perfection, he'd whispered back.

She'd turned on her side, unnoticed while he fixed his gaze to the skies, marveling at the beauty around them...and fell in love, knowing she would one day marry Lord Lucien Jonas.

How very naïve. How very foolish she'd been. Hers had been the wishes of a girl who'd believed the bond between them was so great, that one day he would realize he carried the same love in his heart that she did in hers. She marveled that she'd ever been so blessedly innocent. Eloise tightened her mouth. However, just as he was not the same man, she was not the same woman. She knew with the experience of a woman who carried regrets in her heart that if he did not do this, if he continued to forsake his family for decisions of the past, the burden he carried would be even greater.

Filled with a restive energy, she pushed herself away from the mantel and began to pace the hardwood floors, padding silently back and forth. He would not come. Her naiveté in believing she could sway his opinion, that what they'd once shared as children would be enough to convince him that the hatred he carried in his heart was futile and a waste of good emotion, was staggering.

Her gaze wandered unbidden to the forgotten crumpled sheets of parchment upon her secretaire. She yanked her stare away, refusing to look at the hastily discarded notes.

If she were to reclaim that seat and finish one of those notes, it would be a betrayal Lucien could never forgive, nay would never forgive. This bitter animosity he'd carried since his return from war was testament to that. He'd always been a man who loved passionately, which was splendorous to the recipient of that love. Yet, by the man he'd become, it was clear he felt all emotions with that staggering intensity. If she penned that note, if she did this thing she would relinquish the right to everything they'd shared before.

Eloise pressed her fingers against her temples and rubbed the pained ache of indecision throbbing in her head. She'd never been accused of being selfish before. Not when she'd left the comforts of her own home, a recently wedded young lady, to care for Lucien's wife and son while he was off fighting. Not when she'd stayed beside them, caring for them when the bloody doctor had said nothing else could be done. Not when she'd fallen ill for her efforts.

But in this, she wanted to be selfish. She wanted to cling to the idea that Lucien might, for all the acrimony he carried, come to care for her as he once had. With slow steps, she wandered over to her secretaire and sank onto the delicate, mahogany chair. She slid to the edge and picked up an empty sheet. The moment she put those words to paper the dream of him would be lost to her.

Eloise fisted the edges of the page and closed her eyes drawing in several, slow breaths. Then opened her eyes and set the sheet down. Even as she loved him, he'd never been hers. And she loved him enough that she'd sacrifice their friendship if it meant he could be happy once more.

She plucked the pen from the crystal ink well and proceeded to write.

My Lady Drake...

A knock sounded at the door and her fingers skidded along the page. She dropped the pen, smattering ink upon the vellum. Eloise jumped to her feet as her butler appeared in the doorway, beside the frowning visage of her brother-in-law, and now since her husband's death, the Earl of Sherborne.

"The Earl of Sherborne," the nasal pronouncement of the graying servant filled the quiet.

Eloise bit back a sigh of regret and forced a smile to her lips. "Kenneth," she began.

"Eloise," he stalked into the room as bold as if she were his countess, which she never would have been. She'd not have wedded one such as him, if it would have afforded her the title Queen of England. He paused with the pale pink, upholstered sofa between them and tugged at his lapels. "This is not a matter of a social call," he said coolly.

She sighed. It was to be this manner of visit. Again. By the flush on his hard cheeks and icy cool stare, she'd done something to earn his displeasure. Eloise pasted on a falsely serene smile and inclined her head. "It is ever a pleasure," she lied through her imperfect teeth. "Though I must admit to surprise at your late," as in extremely, unfashionably late, "visit." She waved a hand to the sofa. "Would you care to—?"

"I understand you are a widow, madam, but I have expectations for you."

She narrowed her eyes while fury stirred to life in her belly at his highhandedness. "You have expectations for me?" she asked slowly.

Kenneth jabbed a long finger in the air. "My brother could have wed any young lady." Yes that much had likely been true. Affable and pleasantly handsome, he was everything his brother, the new earl, was not. Then, mayhap it was his rotten soul that was ugly more than anything else. "And he wed you," he snarled that last word allowing her to know exactly what he thought of his late brother's selection in wife.

She bit back the tart words she really wanted to hurl at his face. "I imagine some more pressing matter has brought you 'round than to demean your brother's widow," she said, infusing a droll note into those words that increased the earl's ire.

He opened and closed his mouth like a trout, trying to shake free the metal hook in its mouth. Kenneth rested his hands on the back of the sofa and leaned across. "When my brother set up the magnanimous terms of your betrothal contract," he said with such vitriol she took a step back. "He did not imagine that should anything happen to him, his wife would become such a shameful, scandalous creature."

A shocked gasp burst from her lips.

He continued his stinging diatribe. "The gossip has begun circulating," he hissed. Her body felt awash in shame with the truth she'd been discovered in Lucien's arms, shame which had nothing to do with his station in the marquess' household and everything to do with her longing for a man who would never want her. "You were seen at London Hospital."

"What?" she blurted and blinked at him.

He slashed a hand through the air. "I've learned you were seen visiting London Hospital without a chaperone, paying a visit to men. In their beds."

By God, *this* is what he should find an egregious offense? A hysterical giggle escaped her lips. What would he say if he were to discover she'd been passionately kissing Lord Lucien, a man in the Marquess of Drake's employ? He'd likely find that the kind of offense punishable by hanging. Her giggling increased and she buried it in her hands. Her efforts proved futile as it escaped through her fingers, all the more damning for it being the sole sound in the otherwise silent room.

"Do you find this a matter of humor, Eloise?" his barking question more reminiscent to a stern papa with a recalcitrant child than an annoyed brother-in-law. In fairness, he was a good deal more than annoyed.

Not for the first time since her husband's passing she gave thanks for the magnanimous terms of the contract that had seen her cared for in the unfortunate event of his demise. Modestly comfortable with earnings of one-third of his properties, he'd seen to it that she'd never be dependent upon another man. She was never more grateful than staring at his rabid brother with spittle forming at the corner of his fleshy lips.

"Do you have nothing to say?"

She composed herself, schooling her features into a collected mask that conveyed little, knowing in his inability to do so, he'd only be more infuriated by her response. "There is nothing shameful in my visits to London Hospital."

His blond eyebrows shot to his hairline.

Eloise took a step toward him, emboldened by his silence. "The men there are heroes." And lonely. A prick of needle-like pain stuck in her heart in thinking of Lucien as one of those heroes, alone. The solitary man described by the marchioness and it only fed her infuriation with the earl. "And if it brings them a measure of peace, my being there, then I intend to visit." Her voice increased in volume under the force of her emotion. "Whether or not that offends your sensibilities." Her chest heaved. "Have I made myself clear, my lord?"

He sputtered. "Abundantly." He gave a disgusted toss of his head, dislodging an oiled blond curl over his high brow. "My brother would be ashamed by your ac—"

She cut into his words. "If you believe he would be ashamed by my actions, then you didn't know your brother." Eloise strode to the door. "Now, if you'll excuse me, my lord. It is late." She paused and pasted a hard smile on her lips. "And I have plans for tomorrow morning." That now, in addition to her shameful visit with the marchioness, would first include a visit to London Hospital.

He gave her a long, black look and then stalked out of the room.

The tension went out of her and her shoulders sagged with the weight of relief at his departure. She returned to her secretaire and stared at the black ink marring the page, the three word greeting penned, now undecipherable. Only looking at the blank pages before her, the heinous accusations leveled at her by her brother-in-law infiltrated her thoughts and she could not shake them free. Would her husband have found her actions scandalous? Knowing the supportive man he'd been, she would have wagered all her security as his widow, that he'd have supported any charitable ventures.

Eloise laid her arms upon the table and folded her hands together. What would he have said about her relationship with Lucien, though? She lowered her chin to her hands, her gaze absently trained on the thick, gold brocade curtains. She'd spoken of Lucien to Colin quite frequently. He'd, of course, known the stories of her childhood and part of the affection she'd had for Lucien. Much of the laughter they'd shared had been with the memories she'd imparted of Lucien and his brothers. Her marriage had never possessed the burning love that set hearts afire, but rather kind, comfortable companionship. No, there had been no grand passion between them.

Unlike Lucien.

She pressed her eyes closed. In the time she'd been wed, in all the awkward visits Colin had paid to her bedchamber, her body had never thrilled with desire for his touch.

Then there was Lucien. Their relationship had never been one of volatile emotion. They were merely two emotionally charged persons who'd had a powerful friendship. Never anything more. Just friend-ship. Only…Her lips burned with the memory of his kiss upon her lips, the memory of him forever stamped in her heart, mind, and now body. His commanding possession of her mouth had been no act of a friend.

Then, after what she intended, she would stake all the money left in her dowry that she'd not even have Lucien's friendship.

Eloise picked up the pen once more…and wrote.

NINE

The following afternoon, Eloise stood outside the Marchioness of Drake's townhouse. She'd written the note. Eloise frowned at the door. "It is a good deal harder being furtive when the gentleman in question is in fact—" Her words died as Lucien pulled the door open.

He glared down at her.

—It was a good deal harder to be furtive when the gentleman happened to be the *butler*.

She gave him her winningest, I-do-not-have-any-underhanded-actions-planned-that-will-make-you-hate-me-forever smile and completed her step. "Hullo, Lucien."

"Remember yourself, madam." He gritted his teeth so loud, even with the space between them and the carriage rattling by, she heard the snap of them. He glanced up and down the street and, for the span of a heartbeat, she thought he intended to slam the door in her face. For all his ire with her for making a nuisance of herself, he was first and foremost a gentleman and had a sense of honor where responsibilities and obligations were concerned. He motioned her inside.

A nervous stone settled in her stomach and before her courage deserted her, she sprinted up the steps. "Lucien," she greeted.

The footman who rushed forward to help her out of her cloak paused at the familiarity between her and the head servant. Lucien turned a glower on the handsome, liveried servant who gulped audibly and hurried off with her aquamarine, muslin cloak.

"You needn't be so surly with—"

64

"I'll not have you telling me how to handle my responsibilities." Odd, she should forget he was a servant and not the master of this great home. "Would you have servants gossiping about you?" he demanded on an angry whisper. "Imagine the scandal of the Countess of Sherborne carrying on with the Marquess of Drake's butler."

She considered her brother-in-law, the earl, last evening. Oh, she could very well imagine his outrage. If he'd been foaming at her visits to London Hospital, he'd have suffered an apoplexy for her extreme familiarity with Lucien. She gave a flounce of her curls. "No matter."

He took a threatening step toward her, backing her away. "No matter," he repeated on a menacing whisper.

Her back thumped against the doorframe and she shook her head. The door rattled at her back.

"Why, Eloise? Because you still harbor some illusion that I'm that nobleman's son?"

She pointed her eyes to the ceiling. "Well, you *are* a viscount's son. That can't be undone." No matter how much he wished it. A startled squeak escaped her as he tugged her into an opened room. He closed the door behind them. Had it been anyone other than Lucien, she'd have trembled with terror. She swallowed hard. Even so, he was quite menacing in his ire.

He flexed his jaw. "Do you prefer the viscount's son to the servant, then?"

I prefer you in any way and every way. With one arm, two arms, no arms. "Well, the viscount's son was ever more charming."

His eyebrows dipped in a threatening fashion. It was so very wrong, but she reveled in his absolute lack of control. If he were indifferent toward her, their past, his family, he would be composed and unaffected…and he was not.

Lucien lowered his mouth close to hers and whispered against her lips, "Or perhaps you delight in the prospect of tupping a mere servant."

Eloise slapped him. The force of her blow snapped his head back. The stinging sound of flesh meeting flesh echoed in the corridor.

She widened her eyes. Oh, God, she had hit him. Granted she'd planted him any number of facers when he'd schooled her on lessons of defending herself. "L-Lucien," she whispered and covered her mouth with her palm. But this was different. This was Lucien the man whom she'd missed. He might be a foul fiend now, but for everything that had come before, he did not deserve her violence.

He touched his fingers hesitantly against the mark she'd left upon his skin and flexed his jaw several times.

She shook her head. "I am so sorry," she said on a rush, not because she feared him but because she'd struck him. Even if he had deserved it, she still would never inflict hurt—He'd certainly known enough of that. "I…"

A slow grin turned his lips up. Not the vicious, angry sneers he'd bestowed upon her too many times in a mere handful of days, but a true smile that reached his eyes. The silver flecks danced in the gray-blue depths. He was mad. There was no accounting for his unexplainable humor. "I find some reassurance in knowing you put the lessons I gave you through the years to good use."

She smiled. "You remember that?"

Lucien chuckled. "Remember allowing you to slap me and punch me to be sure you knew how to properly defend yourself?" He touched his cheek once more. "Yes, I remember that well." His hand fell back to his side and his smile died, replaced by the unyielding, black look perpetually worn by him. "Have you had need of the lessons I imparted?"

She shivered at the lethal edge to the question that promised harm to any man who may have been the recipient of her wrath. "No, Lucien," she assured him. "I've lived quite an uneventful, staid life of a wedded young lady and now a widow." Her breath caught as he touched an unexpected hand to her cheek, cupping the flesh.

"And are there no scoundrels who've made a nuisance of themselves for a place in your bed?" He ran his thumb over her lower lip.

Her lips parted under the slight gesture. It was a seductive, teasing caress. Yearning for more, his kiss, more of his touch robbed her of practical thoughts and logic. What had he said? She tried to drum up an answer to his question. "I am not the scandalous sort, Lucien," she said at last, finding an answer. "I never have been." She couldn't keep the trace of hurt from those four words. With everything Lucien knew about her, how could he believe her capable of such indecency?

Lucien continued to move his coarse, callused thumb higher. He gently rubbed the birthmark at the edge of her lip. "Ah, but that's not what I asked."

"Wh-what did you ask?" Her head fell back, knocking noisily against the door, and she tried desperately to dredge forth that question that had so offended.

"I asked if there were scoundrels vying for a place in your bed."

She wet her lips and his gaze dipped, following that slight movement. "I'm a widow, Lucien." For the limited interest she'd received when she'd made her Come Out, the moment she'd come out of mourning, she'd been besieged by a sea of suddenly interested, eager gentleman who desired nothing more than a "place in her bed" as Lucien so succinctly put it.

The grays of his eyes darkened, very nearly black. "Mr. Jones," he corrected.

She frowned. "Your name isn't Jones and I won't call you that. You are Lord Lucien Jonas and that is who you'll always be." He continued to study her through his thick, hooded gaze. At one time she'd known his thoughts better than she'd known even her own. Now, she probed, searching for hint of what he was thinking.

He wanted to kill every bloody bastard who'd dared put an indecent offer to her.

Wanted it with the same, savage ferocity that had driven him to bloodlust in the thick of battle, an overwhelming, almost crippling sentiment that had nothing to do with the girl Eloise had been and everything to do with the woman she'd become.

And worse…the man he now was.

Lucien took in her full, red lips wondering at the men who'd also kissed her lips. Whole men. Gentlemen. Noblemen with intact limbs and unscarred bodies. Men who'd never entertained such vile, cowardly thoughts as ending their own lives and who'd languished in a hospital for years, willing themselves to die.

For the first time, he wanted to be whole again. For her.

"I used to know what you were thinking," Eloise confided softly. "No more."

"What I'm thinking would have you wilting in this parlor," he said with a matter-of-factness that brought her lips down in a small frown.

She squared her shoulders. "I'm far more resilient than you'd take me for."

A snide contradiction hovered on his lips, but something gave him pause, and he called the words back. A mature glint to her eyes, eyes that once had bore an innocence he'd shared in as a child. Yes, it seemed life had happened to Ellie, too. It wasn't his business, and yet for some inexplicable reason, he needed to know. "And have you taken a lover?" he asked with a bluntness that brought a crimson blush to her cheeks. That blush also served as an answer more powerful than a thousand words. A woman capable of that telling, innocent gesture had not accepted any of those indecent offers. Some of the tension eased from his frame.

"No," she said, confirming his silent supposition. She stroked his jaw, the sweetly, soothing gesture brought his lids closed, feeding a hunger he'd not realized he'd had for a warm, gentle touch. *This* touch. Eloise's touch. "I am lonely." Her wrenching admission brought his eyes open. "Yet even in my loneliness, I crave more than that empty meeting of two people."

He knew that same loneliness. Had known it since he returned from the Continent to confront a life in which the only person who'd sustained him through countless battles, was dead and gone, and with her, the son he'd never known. Only in this moment, with Eloise here, for the first time, he didn't feel alone. Lucien knew better than to ask dangerous questions that would only yield more dangerous answers. "What do you crave?" And yet, the question came anyway.

A wistful smile hovered on her lips. "You still don't know, do you?" she said, a quiet awe underscoring that question.

He stiffened.

She shook her head. "You never really saw me, did you?"

A blinding panic built inside his chest as he sought for words to stop the flow of the admission on her lips.

"You never realized that I loved you."

Oh, God.

He staggered away from her. His heart thumped loudly, deafeningly in his ears, drowning out logic and reason and leaving him with a numbing dread to the implications of Eloise's declaration.

She stepped away from the door, and advanced toward him. And God help him, he'd have chosen to face down Boney himself again and all his armies on the fields of battle than this young woman who'd have him reenter a world he no longer belonged in. "I don't expect those words from you, Lucien," she said pragmatically. "I know your heart was and forever will belong to Sara, but I wished I'd told you, even as I would have humbled myself at the feet of a man who loved another, because then mayhap when you returned from battle and found your wife and child gone, you'd have known there was another who desperately loved you and ached to help you resume living."

"Stop." The plea tore from him, desperate and hoarse. He didn't want to imagine a world with Eloise silently loving him and him having so callously forgotten her. He was shamed by the wrongs he'd committed in dismissing her from his life.

Eloise proved more relentless than Wellington's soldiers at Waterloo, continued walking and stopped when the tips of their feet brushed. "And I know what happens from here, you'll forever resent me for it, but know I did everything I did for that love of you." She inclined her head. "Now, I really must see the marchioness."

He managed a jerky nod, even as her words confounded him. He focused on the overwhelming relief of the pardon and he spun on his heel. He didn't wait to see if she followed, knowing from the soft tread of her satin-slippered feet that she followed him from the parlor and trailed behind at a sedate, respectable pace. Lucien was never more grateful to step foot into another parlor. He cleared his throat. "The Countess of Sherborne," he said coolly.

The marchioness seated at the windowseat with a book on her lap, glanced up. She smiled and moved her gaze between him and Eloise. Never more had he resented his new post in the marquess' household, being made an object of scrutiny to Eloise. If he were still the viscount's son, he would have wheeled around and left. Instead of this pained, prolonged moment of waiting to be dismissed.

"That will be all, Jones," the marchioness said, politely inclining her head.

Lucien gritted his teeth. He should be glad to be well-rid of Eloise and the memories she represented. Yet, what was this niggling deep inside to remain precisely where he was and damn the marchioness' orders to the Devil?

What in the hell?

Eloise stepped into the room, her impossibly large eyes trained on him and as he took his leave, he rather thought fighting down those bloody Frenchmen on the field of battle would be preferable to facing these two determined women.

TEN

Eloise stared at the door Lucien had just fled through. He may as well have been a stranger to her now, with a gaping hole in the years of their friendship, but she well knew the look of horror she'd roused in his eyes with her admission. Hurt and fury warred for supremacy with outrage ultimately triumphing. How dare he treat her as though she were nothing more than a stranger? Why, if he returned, by God she'd clout him upon his head.

"Would you care to sit?" Emmaline questioned softly.

She jumped and flushed, turning her attention to the oft-smiling marchioness. "Uh, yes, thank you." The woman eyed her with a knowing gleam in her kindly eyes. Eloise claimed a seat on the powder blue sofa, reminded once more of the horrible person she herself was because of the niggling resentment that settled in her heart. The marchioness' presence had pulled Lucien back from the pit of despair...when Eloise hadn't been even a memory he'd carried.

She ran her fingers over the rose etched in the blue upholstery, the pale hue putting her in mind of that sky she and Lucien had once gazed at. Eloise picked her gaze up and found Emmaline patiently waiting. She forced her fingers to cease their distracted movement "I do not know if you remember what I'd mentioned several days ago." She looked to the doorway, ascertaining he was truly gone and then shifted her attention to Emmaline. "About Lucien...Lieutenant Jonas...*Jones*," she corrected a third time.

Emmaline glided over. Her sapphire blue skirts rustled as she claimed the spot beside Eloise. "I remember any number of things you shared with me." She waited and gave an encouraging nod.

"About..." Aware of a sudden of the volume of her voice, Eloise spoke in a hushed whisper. "Lieu...oh bother, would you be horribly scandalized and outraged if I were simply to refer to him by his Christian name?" she asked, never one to prevaricate.

A little laugh escaped the other woman. "Not at all. I imagine having been acquainted as children you are entitled that freedom."

"Yes, I suppose you are indeed correct." Eloise liked the marchioness more and more. And with every word to leave her lips, Emmaline chipped away at the unfair jealousy she'd carried since learning of Lucien's relationship with the lovely woman. "I had mentioned that a familial matter brought me here." Which was largely true, but not totally true. Her love had driven her search and determined effort to find him. She drew in a slow breath and tried to dredge up the words.

How could she try and force his hand in this manner? She looked down at a wrinkle in her skirts that traversed a path from her upper thigh to her knee. Nor was Lucien's story hers to tell.

"What is it?" Emmaline encouraged quietly.

"His father is ill," she said finally, settling for the simplest truth. "The viscount—"

Emmaline's eyes formed moons in her face. "The *viscount?*"

"I believed you knew." Guilt twisted even greater at unwittingly betraying his secret. "His father is a viscount."

The marchioness sat back in her chair, flummoxed. She shook her head. "I assure you, we did not." By the troubled glimmer in the marchioness' kind, brown eyes, Eloise suspected Lucien would have never been given his current post had that truth been known. Steward to the marquess, perhaps. But never, butler.

She bit the inside of her cheek. Oh God, he would never forgive her. But worse, if he did not journey to Kent once more and have his parting with his father, he'd never forgive himself. This betrayal of sorts was an attempt on her part to put to rights his broken family. Coming here, to this household had never been about Eloise or the dream of more with Lucien. It had only been about him. "His father is dying." Pain suffused her heart at the reminder that the viscount, the garrulous, smiling man she'd known since she was a child, was nearing the end of his days.

Emmaline pressed her hands against her cheeks. "Oh." That single syllable utterance conveyed all the depth of painful emotion known by a woman who'd also known loss. It was not, however, Eloise's place to delve into the loss she herself had known.

They spoke simultaneously.

"He must go see him."

"He will not go see him."

Their words ran together, and perhaps it was the jumbled confusion of their blended voices or perhaps it was shock at Eloise's words, but the marchioness widened her eyes and said, "Beg your pardon?"

She treaded carefully, seeking to divulge only the details she must. Though no matter what paper and ribbon were selected to dress it up, a betrayal was a betrayal. "It is not my place to share Lucien's history, but strife between them came when the viscount insisted on his youngest son," she paused remembering belatedly this woman, for all she did know of Lucien, didn't know all the parts of his life, the way Eloise did. "Lucien wanted to join the clergy. His father insisted he follow the drum." She moved her attention away from the other woman and her gaze collided with an urn filled with flowers.

"What happened?"

Those cheerful, delicate blooms served as a mark of cheer upon Eloise's dark thoughts. The white daisies within the arrangement beckoned, and she stood and wandered over. She leaned down and inhaled the sweet, fragrant scent that transported her to fields of spring flowers.

I am quite cross with you, Lucien. You were to help me pick flowers and... And that was the last he'd ever picked a flower with her. Or walked with her. Or teased her. "He fell in love," her voice, the faintest whisper. She straightened, glancing over her shoulder at Emmaline.

The marchioness stared at her with wide, tragic eyes. "Oh, Eloise." She gave her a sad smile. "You love him."

Tears filled her eyes and she blinked back the useless tears of weakness. Emmaline's words merely served to bring her to the purpose in coordinating their first meeting and coming here this day. "He is quite obstinate."

"Indeed he is."

"He'll not come merely because I ask it, or because he should."

Understanding dawned in the other woman's brown eyes. "Ahh."

Eloise hurried over, her skirts snapping wildly at her ankles. "He will not listen to me." She sank into the seat beside Emmaline. At one time he would have. No longer. "If you reasoned him out of London Hospital, my lady, then you can convince him to make this journey with me."

Emmaline said nothing for a very long while and Eloise suspected she didn't intend to help, thought she might gently, but politely, beg to not interfere in personal matters that did not belong to her. But then, she nodded slowly. "I imagine if I cannot see he makes this important journey, my husband will."

Her eyes slid closed on a wave of gratitude. "Thank you."

"Oh, don't thank me," she said dryly. "I've not accomplished anything yet. And knowing your Mr. Jones as I do, if he does not wish to make this journey, well then it will not be an easy task for either me *or* my husband to accomplish."

Eloise opened her eyes and looked to Emmaline. She shifted under the weight of the marchioness' scrutiny.

Then Emmaline asked, "How long have you loved him?"

"All of my life," she said softly, remembering back to the day she'd first met Lucien and his brothers. Her father and the viscount, owners of property in the same county, had been fast friends from their youth. A wistful smile tugged at her lips. "Well, not my whole life. We were, however, children when we first met." The hard, angry frown an adult Lucien had turned on her moments ago bore traces of the child's frown he'd worn at their first meeting. "His father gave him the task of playing with me." Her lips pulled in remembrance of that long ago day; the fire in his gray-blue eyes, the tight set to his angry mouth. "Needless to say, he resented being made to play with a small girl."

Curiosity lit the other woman's eyes. "What did you do?"

She grinned. "I punched him."

Emmaline's laughter echoed off the high-ceilings and plastered walls. "I imagine that did not earn you a friend in Mr. Jones."

"Oh, no, you're wrong, my lady." Eloise shook her head. "He accused me of punching like a lady and took it upon himself to instruct me on the proper way to plant one a facer." From that point, he'd become her best friend—whether he wanted her friendship or not. Then, he'd welcomed her friendship. She caught her lower lip between her teeth and worried the flesh. Now was an altogether different tale.

The marchioness placed a hand on Eloise's and she started. The woman held her stare and then said, "I visited Jones for several years... and upon each of my visits, he never opened his eyes. He would sit with his face directed at the window, but his eyes closed. I despaired of ever seeing them. I sometimes wondered if he were incapable of opening them...and yet, one day, he just..." Her expression grew far-off. "He just opened his eyes," she repeated. "I believe he will open them once more, Eloise. I truly do."

Not after this. Not after her great interference in his contented life. "Thank you, my lady," she said, not able to contradict the erroneous claim.

"Emmaline," the woman graciously reminded her.

"Emmaline," she murmured. And as Eloise took her leave a short while later, she felt the first stirrings of hope.

ELEVEN

Lucien stared at the Marquess of Drake's closed office door. He'd been summoned. And he rather suspected he very well knew what this particular meeting was about—the steward's position in the country.

His mind had shied away from anything and everything that reminded him of Sara. The wife he'd loved and the happy life he'd imagined for them, belonged in the past. Yet, the post dangled responsibility in the respected position using his mind for business matters, a task he'd enjoyed once upon a lifetime ago, before he'd killed too many men on the fields of battle. Accepting the position would also mean he'd be free of Eloise, who'd inserted herself so effortlessly, so seamlessly, into his life. Eloise who, with her kiss and words of love, made him hunger for...more.

He raised his hand to knock. Then froze.

If he accepted the position, he'd never see her again. There would be little chance or need of the Countess of Sherborne to visit the marquess' country landholdings in Leeds. By all rights, that very truth should have easily sealed his decision. He closed his eyes tight. But by God, now that she'd reentered his life, he could not imagine a world in which she was no longer in it.

Lucien squared his jaw. And yet that great sacrifice would maintain the walls he'd erected about his heart, to keep him safe. He rapped once.

"Enter," the marquess' deep baritone carried through the thick panel.

Lucien pressed the handle and entered. "Captain," he greeted. "You wanted to see me?"

The other man looked up, something, an emotion very nearly pity and regret flashed in his eyes. "Yes, come in," he said quietly, motioning him forward. "Please, close the door."

Lucien hesitated a moment, the first stirrings of unease traversed a path along his spine. He closed the door and it clicked shut. He turned to face his employer and a sudden, horrifying niggling entered his thoughts. Did the marquess know Lucien had kissed Eloise, the marchioness' guest not once, but twice and very nearly a third time this afternoon when she'd arrived? His neck heated with shame and he resisted the urge to tug at his suddenly too-tight cravat.

Lord Drake shoved back his chair. Wordlessly, he crossed around his desk and walked with purposeful strides to the sideboard in the corner. He picked up a decanter of whiskey and pulled off the stopper. "Would you care for a drink?" He splashed several fingersful into a glass.

"No, thank you, Captain," he said.

The marquess was a man of honor. A gentleman who'd not tolerate his servants, even if they had served under him on the battlefields, to go about kissing his wife's company. His stomach muscles clenched involuntarily at the horrifying prospect of losing his post. After years of living in a depressed state and resisting the urge to kill himself, he'd found purpose. He couldn't lose this stability.

"As you're aware, Lady Sherborne visited with my wife this afternoon."

The pressure built inside his chest. He nodded slowly. "I'm aware of that, Captain," he said cautiously.

The marquess carried his glass over to his desk and propped his hip against the edge. "Why, don't you sit, Jones?" He waved his glass, motioning to the leather winged back chair at the foot of his desk.

Lucien hesitated and then with wooden movements, crossed over and took the proffered seat. Nausea churned in his belly. Since he'd fled Kent, thin, haggard and broken, he'd handled himself with an unflappable composure. Or he had. Until that blasted momentary loss of sanity in his employer's foyer just a short while ago. With his lone hand, he tightly gripped the arm of his chair.

Lord Drake swirled the contents of his glass and then took a sip. "The Viscount Hereford is your father," he said without preamble.

Lucien blinked. "Captain?" The question emerged haltingly as he tried to piece together not only the marquess' discovery but also his interest in Lucien's origins.

The other man took another sip and then set his glass down beside him with a soft thunk. "Surely you didn't believe that I believed with your bought commission of lieutenant that you were not of some means."

He narrowed his eyes. By God this was not about his kissing Eloise until she was pliant in his arms.

…I know what happens from here, you'll forever resent me for it, but know I did everything I did for that love of you…

"I'm not of some means," he said coolly. By God…Eloise! A slow, seething rage fanned out. He balled his hand into a fist. A muscle jumped in his jaw.

"Very well, then you didn't believe you came from means? It's the same, though isn't it, Jones?" he said pragmatically.

"It isn't."

"It is not my right to pry into your past."

Then don't. Lucien snapped his teeth together hard, gritting them to keep from hurling those disrespectful words at the man, who with his wife, had breathed life into him once again.

"I blamed my father for my enlistment," Drake said quietly. As though filled with a sudden disquiet, the other man picked up his glass. He stared into the half-filled contents, seeing a world that only existed behind his eyes. Though Lucien ventured he knew a good deal about those visions there.

"Captain?" They were the kind of memories that robbed you of sleep and stole your sanity with one loud sound that transported you to the bloody battlefields.

The marquess gave his head a shake and took another sip. "It was the height of immaturity to enlist. I resented my betrothal to Emmaline and sought to escape my father's domineering control of my life." His lips twisted in a hard, bitter smile. "Yet, ultimately it was my decision. I spent years hating my father. Hating myself."

Lucien well knew that. He lived with that very same hatred. Perhaps every man who returned did.

"It took my wife to teach me that hate is futile and useless. We lived, when others died…and to live our lives full of loathing and bitterness is a waste of that life."

"You have a reason to live," Lucien spat. The marquess hadn't lost his wife and child.

Lord Drake shifted his hip. "I imagine you do, as well. If you'd but see it." With that, he shoved himself up from his reclined position and carried his glass behind his desk. "I'm giving you three weeks."

He shook his head slowly, uncomprehendingly. "I don't—?"

"You're welcome to a horse in my stables and a carriage." He sat in his leather seat, the aged chair crackled noisily. "Go see your father, Jones."

It wasn't a suggestion. The marquess commanded with the same decisive firmness he'd evinced on the battlefield.

He gave his head a jerky shake.

"I'm not asking you," the marquess confirmed that which Lucien had already suspected.

Rage thrumming through his body, filled his legs and brought him upright. He paced in front of the immaculate, mahogany desk. "I have a new life. I have responsibilities—"

"And the under butler will see to those obligations while you're gone," the marquess assured.

He raked a shaking hand through his hair. He'd not seen his brothers and father in five, almost six, years. But for the one volatile visit when he'd first returned, he'd stormed out, made for London and never looked back. The stricken expressions on his brothers' faces— faces so similar to his own, as young men—it had been the same as looking into a mirror.

Only the glass had cracked and he was now the distorted, amorphous figure on the other side of that bevel glass. His father's insistence had ultimately plunged Lucien into hell. His brothers, however, their only crime was reminding him of what had once been and what would never again be.

He shook his head again, this time slower with more precise movements. "I won't go, my lord." He paused and fixed a hard stare on his employer. "You'll have to sack me."

A wry grin formed on the marquess' lips. "You know me enough to know by now I won't sack you."

A momentary relief surged through him.

Lord Drake quelled that elusive feeling with his next words. "But neither are you permitted to stay here for three weeks." He waved a hand. "If you'll not go, then take yourself somewhere where you can think clearly and logically, and then hopefully that time to reflect brings you back home."

Before it is too late. The words hovered, unspoken in the air between them.

The set, imperturbable lines of the marquess' face proved that, once more, Lucien had been robbed of choice yet again. "Is there anything else you require?" The question emerged harsher than he intended...or could help.

Lord Drake shook his head.

With a curt bow, Lucien took his leave, closing the door behind him.

Goddamn you, Eloise. Goddamn you.

TWELVE

A loud bang jerked Eloise upright. She squinted in the dimly lit room, trying to make the numbers out on the ormolu clock atop her mantel. Ten o'clock in the evening. Quiet descended upon her chambers once more and giving her head a shake, she settled back to continue reading.

Angry shouts and her usually stoic butler's stammering cries penetrated the perceived peace. Eloise set aside her book of Coleridge's poems and flung her legs over the side of the bed. She dragged on her modest robe at the foot of her bed, concealing her equally modest nightshift.

Whatever...? If it was her blasted brother-in-law with his zealous opinions about her actions and inactions, she'd have him tossed on his ear this time, she would. She pulled the door open and started down the corridor. With every step she took, Forde's shouts grew frenzied in volume and passion.

"How dare you, sir? Her Ladyship is—"

"Oh, she'll receive me, Goddamn it."

Her feet drew to a sudden halt at the familiar, gruff baritone. She widened her eyes. Oh, dear.

"Find her now."

For one moment of sheer cowardice, she cast a longing glance down the corridor toward the safety and peace of her chambers.

"If you do not leave this instant," Forde rumbled, "I will have you forcibly removed."

That threat propelled her forward. Eloise sprinted the remaining length of the corridor and halted at the top of the stairwell. She rested a trembling hand along the top rail. As if he felt her presence, Lucien looked up, volatile rage simmering in his eyes. She chewed her lower lip a moment and then managed a forced smile. "H-hello." She gave a halfhearted wave. "S-so lovely of you to call."

The butler, Forde, stared up at her as though she'd sprouted wings and intended to fly the distance down to the front entrance.

Lucien took a step forward, effortlessly striding past the ineffectual, aging butler. "This is no social call." That seething whisper carried in the generous foyer like a shot in the dead of night.

She bit back a sigh. First her horrid brother-in-law, now her long ago friend. Did no one pay social calls, anymore? "Oh." She took a tentative step, pausing at the top step. "Then perhaps we might wait until the morn—?"

"Oh." Poor Forde. He gulped nervously.

She took pity on the graying servant who'd likely just added a handful of additional silver streaks to his coarse hair. "Forde, it is quite all right," she assured him. Or lied. By the seething tension emanating from Lucien's taut frame, she rather suspected it was not at all...all right.

The loyal servant hesitated.

She gave him a reassuring smile and with that, he moved with stiff steps...until Eloise and Lucien were—alone. "You do know you really shouldn't come around at this late hour frightening my servants, Lucien. It isn't at all well-done of you."

"I don't give a damn what it is," he hissed, rocking forward on the balls of his feet as though he were one wrong comment from her away from stalking up the stairs.

She swallowed hard. "I gather you are here following a conversation you had with the marquess." Her fingers quaked in an involuntary tremble and she buried them within her dressing gown to keep from revealing her unease.

His black eyebrows met in a punishing line.

Oh, dear, he was a good deal more menacing than she recalled. She mustered a smile. "I take it he was as supportive and kind as the papers purported him to be."

And that proved to be the one Eloise-comment that set his feet into motion. He boldly climbed the stairs as effortlessly as if he were the master of her modest townhouse—a role she'd gladly have him in forever. She scrambled backward. Well, mayhap not in this icy, domineering role he'd assumed since he'd terrified poor Forde. "What are you doing?" she asked as he continued his slow, menacing climb.

His silence was all the more infuriating. And terrifying. Her heart hammered hard and she retreated another step. She didn't believe he'd hurt her, but his unpredictability made him dangerous. Her heel caught the hem of her robe and she teetered precariously.

She threw her arms out searching for purchase when Lucien closed the distance, easily catching her to him. He folded his arm about her and braced her against his chest. "You bloody fool. Are you trying to break your neck?"

Oh help her. Her eyes slid closed of their own volition and she soaked in the comforting feel of his form pressed to hers. Until she left this Earth she would recall the moment—his powerful body strong, powerful, heated. "Wh-why would I try to break my neck? That's utter nonsense." Her weak-hearted attempt at levity did little to diminish the hardness in his dark gray, now very nearly black, eyes. "Perhaps we should meet in my receiving room?"

He jerked and it was the moment he remembered himself. As a butler in the Marquess of Drake's employ, he likely knew the frequent gossip to fly about a household. Lucien gave a brusque nod, setting her away from him.

Eloise led the way down the stairs, through the foyer, and down the darkened corridor lit by but a handful of sconces to the receiving room. Lucien trailed behind, remarkably stealthy for one of his commanding size. So much so that she shot a quick glance over her shoulder to be sure he still followed. Fury marked his face and she gulped hard. *This is Lucien.* Her dearest friend. Once closer than any two souls could be. He'd never harm her. His low growl echoed behind her. She jumped and quickened her strides. Then, he was in many ways a stranger now.

As they entered the handsomely decorated room with Chippendale furniture, she closed the door softly behind them, knowing her efforts at privacy were futile. She had little doubt that word of this scandalous nighttime visitor would reach her brother-in-law's condescending ears. "I understand you are upset," she said, speaking to him the way she had her mare after the poor creature had injured his front hoof.

He matched her steps. "I am not upset," he whispered.

Eloise hurried to place much needed distance between them. Her shoulders sagged under the weight of her relief. She smiled. "Splendid, then! I—"

"I'm livid."

She flattened her lips. "Oh." Eloise raced behind the rose-inlaid, rectangular table and placed her palms upon the surface. "I needed to reason with you."

Lucien continued coming and stopped at the opposite end of the table and leaned across. "But you didn't reason with me, did you? You forced my hand."

Eloise removed her hands and made to step back. "I can explain." Guilt needled at her conscience once more. She really was very justified in her actions, if he'd but listen.

"There is nothing to explain, madam." A gasp escaped her as he shot his hand out and captured her wrist, halting her flight. Her skin tingled at the power of his hard, callused palm upon her skin. She closed her eyes a moment. Not once in all the years that her husband had come to her chambers had she burned from his touch. She'd believed herself incapable of passion and never expected to know the thrill of desire. Until she'd again found Lucien and had at last known his kiss…and his touch.

"What, do you have nothing to say?" he jeered.

How very humbling it was to ache for a person so wholly unaffected by you. Forcibly she thrust aside any and all weakness, knowing she required strength in this exchange. "I had no other choice," she said, angling her chin up.

Lucien moved a cold stare over her face and then with a black curse that scorched her ears, swiftly released her. "My family is not your business, Eloise," he said, this time there was no lethal edge to his words, but rather a matter-of-factness that was all the more painful for it.

"No, they are not my business," she said softly. "They are like my family." With her father's death the same year Lucien had gone off to fight, the bond between she and Lucien's brothers had only been strengthened. They'd sustained each other, offering and providing solace in some of those darkest times.

Lucien strode around the table and held a finger up. "Ah, yes." He paused, then stopped so close she was forced to crane her head back to meet his gaze. "But they actually are *my* family."

She flinched. When had he become so cruel? Had it been the years of fighting? Perhaps he would have returned this same cynical, wary man to his wife and child. Her heart spasmed. No, their love would have restored him to who he'd been. By the expectant glint in his eyes, he anticipated her volatile outburst. Tears, even. She'd not rise to his bait. Instead, she claimed his hand and held it between her own. "I am glad you at last remembered that important fact, Lucien."

His body jerked erect at her touch. She expected him to wrench his hand free. Instead, he remained rooted to the floor, gaze fixed on her hands twined with his one. The muscles of his throat moved up and down.

A gentle hope stirred in her breast that she'd managed to reason with him. Help him see that for all he'd lost, he still had known love. But for the affection of her doting father, that emotion had been rather sparse in her own life. "Your father loves you," she said. "He—"

Lucien yanked his hand free, shattering the fragile moment of peace between them. He stuck his face close to hers, fury teeming in his eyes. "I lost everything I was, everything I had, because of him." He spun away and she thought he intended to leave, but he merely stalked like a savage beast over to the window. "You live in a world untouched by the horrors of the world, Eloise," he said tiredly. With his disapproving tone he may as well have delivered a gentle rebuke to a child. "With that commission purchased by my father, a path he was determined I take as a third son of little value, I killed men."

She flinched, wanting to stop the flow of his words, but needing to hear the hell he'd endured. "Frenchmen not older than you were when I left gutted by my bayonet. Men I called friends, writhing on the fields of battle with their insides splayed open begging to die…"

Eloise clamped her hands over her ears, but he strode over and, with his hand, removed them, awkwardly clasping them within his grip. "If you are insistent on returning me to the man responsible for the nightmares, then you'll hear it all."

She shook her head, tears clogged her throat, filled her eyes until he blurred before her. "Please."

An ugly grin formed on his lips. "What do you know of it? You never held someone in your arms while they died. You never knew the agony as that person sucked in a final breath and was no more…"

She blinked, fighting to keep from crying, lest he misconstrue her tears as a sign of weakness, but a lone, dratted drop escaped. Followed by another. And another. Until they streamed down her cheeks in a silent, steady torrent. He was wrong. She had known that pain. She'd held Sara and Matthew in her arms and heard that very same uneven, agonizing breath he now described. The memory of that day would forever haunt her. "I know more than you think," she said on a broken whisper.

His lips twisted again in that dark, macabre rending of a smile that spoke more clearly than words his doubts. "I'm returning to see my family. Not because I wish to, but because you willed it. There will be no joyous reunion. There will be no grand showing of remorse and repentance between father and son, if that is what you desire, Eloise." He raked a stare over her that brimmed with resentment and fury. "I leave in the morning and when I return to London, I don't want to see you. I'll resume my responsibilities in the marquess' service and you and I shall continue to move in our different social spheres. I want the memory of you to end with my father. Is that clear?"

Eloise managed a shaky nod. "Yes," she said, amazed that he couldn't hear the cracking of her heart. "Abundantly." He started for the door. She didn't know where she found the courage, but she called out, "Lucien?"

His steps slowed and he turned back to face her.

Eloise wet her lips. "I just thought I should mention I intend to leave in the morning, as well."

"For where?" he blurted, and for that slight moment, there were none of the harsh lines, no frown on his face and he was the Lucien of old.

"Why, for Kent." She cocked her head. "To see your father."

THIRTEEN

She was going to drive him bloody mad. He'd always known it. First when she'd been a girl of six and insisted his toy soldiers dance with her ruffled dolls. Then when she'd insisted on picking flowers in the fields of daisies after they'd gone fishing as children. And now...at his thirty years to her twenty-eight, with her so casually dismissing his rage and cold demands and expressing her intentions to journey to Kent.

"You're mad," he managed to get out.

She pursed her lips. "Indeed, I am. Livid. But I'll not allow that to prevent me from seeing your father once more."

He drew in a breath, counting silently to five. "I meant insane. Bound for Bedlam."

Eloise's eyes formed moons in her face. "Oh." She shook her head. "No, I'm the other type of mad. The angry one."

He felt his lips turning up in a grin and he quickly suppressed it, refusing to allow Eloise and her charming mouth and sweet spirit to overshadow her betrayal.

She folded her arms mutinously over her chest, plumping the lush mounds of her breast, drawing his attention downward. "And I'll have you know, despite your displeasure, I intend on going."

Lucien tried to process her words. He really did. However, the burning rage that had driven him to her doorstep and into her townhouse like a madman receded under the sudden realization that nothing but a thin robe and nightshift shielded her slender but generously curved body from his gaze.

"Did you hear me?" she snapped, her bosom moved up and down with the force of her breathing.

He stared transfixed by the ethereal sight of her, bathed in the faint candle's glow. When had Eloise Gage grown from the stubborn, wild child running the hills of Kent to…this enticing, captivating creature with a woman's curves and a siren's mouth?

She waved a hand in front of his face. "Hullo, Lucien." Fire snapped in her eyes.

The one constant for Eloise would appear to be the whole stubborn business. He shot his arm around her waist and angled her body close to his. A startled squeak escaped her as he angled her body close. "You always did interfere, didn't you," he whispered against her temple.

She frowned up him. "I prefer to think of it as helping."

"It isn't. A help," he clarified, lest any doubt remain.

The muscles of her throat moved and he took in the length of her graceful neck. He'd never before found a neck as a thing of beauty. Quite practical and not at all sexual, there was something wholly enticing about the graceful length of Eloise's. "Wh-what are you d-doing?" she whispered.

Going mad right alongside you. Lucien groaned and crushed her lips under his, swallowing her breathless moan with his. He slanted his mouth over hers again and again until she whimpered. She reached her arms up and twisted her fingers in his hair, tugging his head forcefully down, better opening herself to his kiss.

He deepened the kiss, giving her what she craved, his tongue engaged in a wild thrust and parry that evoked erotic images, all of which involved Eloise stretched on her back, arms up, legs open. Lucien dragged his mouth away, to her groan of protest, but he merely shifted his lips to the wildly beating pulse in her neck. He nipped and sucked at the delicate flesh that had so enticed. Her head fell back and a small, keening cry escaped her.

He looped his arm about her lithe form, never mourning the loss of his arm more than he did in the moment. The empty place his forearm used to be fairly itched with a hungering to hold her, drag her close and use both arms as he longed to, exploring every curve and contour of her body.

"Lucien," she whispered.

Just that. His name. His name uttered on a hungry, whispering moan jerked him back to the moment. He set her away so quickly she stumbled back. Desire clouded the blue-green of her eyes, turning them a cobalt blue. She blinked. Panic built in his chest. "This will not happen again."

"Why?" She may as well have been asking the time of day or for tea and biscuits as calm as that one word utterance was.

Yes, why not? A traitorous voice inside his head chimed in agreement.

He steeled his jaw. "I've already told you, Eloise. After I've visited my father, I'll return to my life and you'll return to yours. And this," whatever madness now gripped them both, "will be forgotten."

She settled her hands on her hips in her resolute I've-made-up-my-mind-and-you-have-no-other-choice way of hers. "You will join me on the journey?" she said in a question that was not at all a question.

"Will I...?" He closed his mouth and counted once more to five, praying for patience. "No, I will not join you on your journey. You are not going."

She pointed her eyes to the ceiling, similar to the way she'd done as a young girl trying to convince a fifteen year old boy there was nothing more natural in the world than partnering a young lady in the steps of the scandalous waltz as set out by her damned tutors. "I'm going," she said. "I intend to leave at first light." She gave a toss of her head. A single blonde curl fell over her eye. "After all, I'm a widow now, Lucien. I'm permitted certain liberties."

With her pledge, all she forced him to consider was her setting out on the damned roads without a chaperone, with no company but perhaps that of a lady's maid and mayhap a strapping footman. He frowned.

"What are you thinking?" she asked, angling her head.

Except, by her aging butler's total lack of ability at tossing him out on his ear as he'd surely deserved, as a member of the marquess' staff himself, he had to admit that the lack of footmen to protect and defend their mistress from a furious gentleman did not speak volumes of their capability. With a growl, he spun on his heel and marched to the door once more.

The rustle of skirts indicated that she gave chase. "What—?"

"I intend to ride. You shall remain in your carriage and beyond that, I'll have nothing else to do with you or your interfering," he directed that to the doorway. With that, he stalked from the room. The skin of his neck burning from her stare trained on his retreating frame.

Eloise stared after Lucien. She touched her fingers to her mouth. Her lips still burned with the taste of his kiss, her flesh throbbed to know more of his touch. In all her greatest dreams of him, she'd imagined a life that included him in it. A life where he viewed her as more than the childhood friend who'd kept stride with him and his brothers. The day he'd fallen in love with Sara, half of Eloise's heart had died. The other half had lived, in the hope that one day he would at last realize she was there.

Then the muscles of her stomach knotted. Even with the passion between them, and the now three times he'd taken her in his arms, he still did not belong to her.

Eloise sat with shaky legs into the nearest seat, sinking into the stiff folds of the pink satin sofa. Worse, he despised her. Blamed her for trying to restore the loving relationship he'd once known with his family. She stared down absently at her lap. However, he spoke with all the passionate ire of a man who still had family. Yes, he'd lost Sara and his child and that loss would forever haunt him. But for the loss, he still had Palmer, Richard, and, for now, his father.

She had come to appreciate in the aftermath of her father's death and then the sudden loss of her own husband just how alone she was. Her world once full of those who cared had become remarkably empty, leaving her with nothing more than a disapproving brother-in-law for occasional company. No, Lucien was not alone. He'd merely chosen to subsist in a state of solitude. She firmed her lips. He might resent her, even hate her for her interference in his life, but her actions were driven by love for him…and his family. If she could somehow bring him together with his brothers, then the total loss of him from her life would cripple her, but would bring her some measure of peace in her rather lonely life.

Only, if she were being truthful with at least herself, she wanted more. She wanted him.

FOURTEEN

The following morning, with her trunks loaded into a waiting carriage, Eloise accepted the proffered hand of a waiting servant. She gave a murmur of thanks and paused in the threshold of the doorway to survey the quiet streets. The same niggling fear that had danced about her mind all that morning while her belongings were packed and her carriages readied, resurfaced.

Lucien did not intend to come.

When day broke, she'd convinced herself he would be there. She'd delayed her travels, until she was forced to realize he had changed his mind. A single drop of rain landed on her nose. She brushed it off with the tip of her gloved finger.

"My lady?" the servant asked, concern lacing his question.

She gave a shake of her head and, with a small smile, climbed inside the carriage. The door closed behind her with a soft click. Eloise peeled back the red velvet curtain and stared out at the gloomy London streets. Thick, gray storm clouds hung in the sky, blotting out day's bright light. The impending storm perfectly suited her mood that morning.

The carriage dipped under the weight of her driver climbing onto his perch and then a moment later the carriage rocked forward. She stared out at the pink stucco façade of her townhouse. Except for Colin's passing five years earlier, when she'd retired to the country for her period of mourning, she'd not left her modest, comfortable townhouse.

Palmer had written to her frequently, urging her to visit but the pain of her memories were too great to go back to the place she'd

93

loved, lost, and then suffered the pain of Lucien's loss. A ball lodged in her throat and she swallowed several times, but it remained. How very like this day was to the day Sara had drawn her last breath. Her fever had raged for nearly a week, climbing until delirium replaced sanity, and vacancy replaced knowing in the woman's eyes. For all the doctor's efforts and then Eloise's, ultimately nothing she'd done had mattered. She pressed her eyes tightly closed to blot out the memories, but they'd slipped in and would not relinquish their hold.

Lucien's son had succumbed to the fever that same evening. It had been as though the small, cherub-cheeked babe had decided a world without his mother and father was not a world worth living in.

Eloise released her hold on the curtain and the velvet fabric fluttered into place. She dug her fingers into her temple and rubbed in small, continuous circles. Lucien blamed her for having interfered in his life. As the carriage rattled along the quiet, London streets, carrying her to the Kent countryside, she wondered how much greater that blame would be if he'd known just how greatly she'd failed Sara and his child.

She sighed. It seemed for all her intentions where Lucien was concerned, she was determined to fail him.

She'd waited for him. For the hours Lucien had sat astride a chestnut mount provided by the Marquess of Drake, discreetly out of view of Eloise's servants running back and forth with trunks and then empty arms. She'd always been a perfunctory young girl, expressing annoyance when he'd kept her waiting on several scores. He'd never taken her for a young lady who'd delay her journey by hours.

Then, she exited the townhouse, her small shoulders squared and her chin tilted up. With her poise, she had the gracefulness to rival the queen herself. He ran his gaze down her frame. And in her emerald green cloak, fine fabric of an expert cut highlighting her station, lest he forgot the great divide between them. His breath snagged in his lungs as she accepted the hand of a servant, allowing him to assist her up into the carriage.

Lucien narrowed his eyes on the handsome footman who took her hand in his. Even with the space between them, he would have to be blind to fail to note the lust in the bastard's eyes. By the Devil and all his army of demons, if the man was in his employ he'd have sacked him without a reference for daring to look at Eloise as he now did. *Why should you care? She is not your responsibility. And after this journey, she will be nothing at all to you.*

Just then, Eloise froze, one foot inside her black lacquer carriage. She glanced about and he suspected that he was in fact the person she sought...and worse...her delay was, in fact...because of him.

Her plump, red lips he'd worshiped with his mouth just yesterday turned down in a disappointed frown and then she disappeared inside the coach. Moments later, her carriage rocked forward and continued a rumbling path down the empty London streets.

He nudged his borrowed mount forward and set out after her. This sudden urge to join her inside her fine carriage had nothing to do with the uncharacteristic chill of the spring air. And everything to do with her.

A single raindrop hit his eye. Followed by another. With the reins to his horse gathered in his hand, he pulled the brim of his hat lower but it did little to protect him from the steady rain now streaming down. It ran in cold rivulets down his cheeks. But he no longer felt the chill. Living in the muddied, cold and wet fields of European battle-fields, one tended to no longer feel inconveniences such as a little rain. Lightning streaked across the sky and then the heavens opened up in a torrent of rain.

With a silent curse he kicked his mount forward and followed her as they put the streets of London behind them. The relentless storm soaked his garments. He embraced the discomfort, welcoming the sting of the rain until it chilled him through, leaving him numb for it distracted him from the memory of her hurt last evening.

Last night, when he'd sought her out, he'd done so filled with a fiery rage of having his life dictated for him yet again. And this, in Eloise, the woman he'd considered a great friend, had felt like the very worst sort of betrayal. In the light of this new, gray day with her fast-moving carriage bearing her onward to his family, he was humbled under the realization of just what a foul brute he'd become. That, in matters of betrayal, he'd failed Eloise far more than she'd ever failed him. Loyal and steadfast since they'd first taken an oath of friendship with mud and saliva, he'd repaid that loyalty then…and now…? By shutting her out of his life.

He closed his eyes a moment. Then opened them, blinking back the pouring rain that blurred her carriage. He squinted into the distance and his guilty musings fled. What was her driver thinking? The foolish man sped along at a breakneck speed. Lucien's heart froze as her carriage precariously tilted left and, with a curse, he kicked his mount into a full gallop.

By God, if she broke her Goddamn neck in these muddied roads racing to his father, he'd first off her driver and then kill her all over again for her foolishness.

FIFTEEN

Eloise read the contents of the note in her hand, her stomach churning. She set it aside on the carriage bench, abandoning her efforts. Since she'd been a child, she'd been squeamish in a carriage. Reading only exacerbated the discomfort. She sucked in several slow breaths through her nose. All quite unnatural…and a real bother. She sighed. Regardless, she well knew what the missive from Palmer said. She *also* knew even as neither he nor Richard would ever say anything…they would be disappointed in her inability to sway Lucien's mind.

Of course, they long knew Lucien's obstinacies to know that he'd never welcome interference in his life and when pushed…he merely pushed back, all the harder.

They hit another particularly deep bump in the road and her teeth cracked together. She grunted and gripped the edges of her seat to keep from toppling over.

Bloody hell.

She drew in another shallow breath and pressed her eyes closed to combat the nausea when the carriage lurched to a jarring halt. Eloise pitched forward and crashed against the opposite bench. She blinked, momentarily relieved at the cessation of the infernal motion of the carriage, and then shouts split the quiet.

"What in bloody hell are you doing barreling along these roads in that manner?"

Eloise widened her eyes and felt her heart hammering. She shoved herself upright and scrambled into her seat. She yanked at the curtain hard enough to nearly tear it from its hangings just as Lucien swung his well-muscled leg over the side of an enormous, chestnut mount.

What…?

Damning the steady, pounding rain that blurred the glass window, she shoved the door open. A gust of wind slapped at her face. "Lucien?" she shouted into the howling storm.

He stomped over. His serviceable, black riding boots kicked up mud, splattering his black trousers. With the stinging bite of the cold rain, he must be uncomfortable.

Then she met his gaze.

Correction.

By his black scowl, he wasn't uncomfortable…she swallowed hard—he was furious. Stoic and elegant with his hard, determined footsteps, he may as well have been striding through a ballroom than the old, battered, Roman roads to Kent.

"What in hell are you doing?"

She opened her mouth and then it occurred to her—he spoke to her driver.

"I beg your pardon, you brigand."

Her lips twitched. Sopping as he was, Lucien didn't appear either a viscount's son or a distinguished butler.

Lucien stopped beside her carriage and glared down at the five foot nothing driver guiding the team. "Traveling at this pace, you'll see your mistress with a broken neck," he seethed.

The man opened and closed his mouth, an indignant glint in his rheumy eyes. "I beg your—"

"That will be all," Eloise ordered, her attention on Lucien.

He stiffened at her interruption and turned slowly. "Eloise."

Eloise must appear the lackwit with her body half-inside, half-outside of the carriage and the cold rain battering away at her head and stinging her eyes, but she grinned. "You came."

Lucien swiped his hand over his face and mouthed a silent prayer. He lowered his arm to his side. "Get inside your damned carriage."

Her smile dipped and she bristled at his commanding tone. Why, she was not one of the servants in his staff, answering to him. She was—

"Now," he bit out.

Eloise hastily scurried back inside, which had nothing, absolutely nothing, to do with his angry charge and more to do with the rain. Yes, it was simply an effort to remain dry.

The carriage dipped under his weight as he hefted himself in after her and what had previously been a comfortable, generous space shrunk with his towering figure.

The shock of his presence now absorbed, Eloise registered the absolute chill stinging her skin. She folded her arms across her chest and hugged herself. "L-Lucien," she stammered, her teeth noisily chattering.

His eyebrows dipped.

"Wh-what...?"

He cursed and reached for her. "You are going to catch your death of a chill."

They registered his words as one. Their bodies stilled. She held her palm outstretched. "I'm so sorry," she whispered softly. *Sorry for so much.* For the losses he'd known, for her scheming to reunite his family, for his lost arm, for the years he'd spent in London Hospital, for the loss of their friendship...

Lucien managed a terse nod and then the regret in his eyes lifted, replaced with his earlier outrage. With another black curse he opened the door. "To an inn, man." With that brusque command, he closed the door hard behind him. The carriage rocked forward and resumed its ghastly swaying.

How effortless he assumed command. He would forever be a man of the military. "An inn? Lucien, we must continue on." His father's death was imminent.

He ran a methodical glance up and down, from her tangle of wet, blonde curls to her damp skirts. "Surely you do not intend to travel the remainder of this Godforsaken journey as you are?"

CHRISTI CALDWELL

As if her chilled body required any further reminder of her present state, a shudder raked along her spine. She rubbed her forearms to drive back the gooseflesh dotting her skin.

Lucien shrugged out of his wet cloak and tossed it to the floor. "Here," he ordered as he removed his jacket.

"What are you...?" Her words ended as he effortlessly scooped her onto his lap. And just like that, the nauseating rocking of the carriage, the cold of her body, all faded, replaced with rapidly spreading warmth that just came from being in his arms.

The carriage hit a rut in the road, proving her a liar. Her stomach lurched. She swallowed past the wave of nausea, willing herself to not make a humiliating fool of herself by casting the contents of her stomach at his feet. Another rut. She groaned.

Lucien tipped her chin up and when he spoke, his tone emerged gravelly. "What is it?" he asked, as he worked his gaze over her face.

She managed a shaky nod. The carriage swayed and she closed her eyes, concentrating on her breaths, willing the nausea to abate even just a bit.

He brushed his knuckles over her cheeks and she fluttered her lashes, forcing her eyes open. "You still become ill in a carriage?" There was a wistful note to his words, as though a piece of his past had just revisited him in this moment.

Eloise gave her head a slight shake. "N..." Her stomach pitched. "Yes," she finished on an agonized moan.

Lucien rested his still damp, cool palm against her cheek and turned her gently into his chest. The cool sensation eased some of the nausea, made it bearable so she could focus, if even just a bit, on how absolutely right being in his arms was—a coming home. "You would brave this just for my family."

I would brave this all day, every day just for you. "Yes."

He fell silent and this was not the hostile, tense quiet she'd come to expect of the man who'd taken on employment with the marquess. Rather, it was the peaceful, companionable silence they'd once known. Two friends who knew each other so very well they could finish one another's thoughts.

A fierce wind battered at the carriage door and the conveyance swayed. She bit down hard on her lower lip.

Lucien stroked soothing circles over her back "Easy," he whispered into the crown of her hair.

She sucked in another slow breath. He leaned away and she made a sound of protest, but he merely yanked off his dampened cravat. "What…?"

Lucien pressed it against her forehead, his hand firm and reassuring against her skin. "There," he encouraged. "Does that help?"

Barely at all. And yet to say so would result in the loss of his touch. "Yes, it helps." She laid her cheek against his chest and closed her eyes. His heart thumped hard and steady beneath her ear. How many years had she spent worrying after him, waiting for that dreaded note informing her that Lucien had perished in battle? The pain of that loss would have destroyed her. And so, the Eloise Gage who'd hovered on the threshold of girlhood and woman would lie abed bartering with the Lord. And on her most fearful days, the Devil. In the end it seemed the Devil had won. "I missed you." Her whispered words filled the carriage and, as though nature protested her bold utterance, thunder rumbled in the distance.

"I missed you, too," he said, startling her with the quiet words that rumbled up from his chest.

Eloise battled past the nausea and leaned back. "I venture you didn't even give me a single thought."

A twinge of guilt reflected in the stormy, gray irises of his eyes. She glanced away. She'd not have falsity from him. He stroked his thumb over her lower lip and she stiffened, looking at him once more. "I won't lie to you, Eloise. I didn't think of you in a romantic sense." She winced and her body burned with mortification, driving back the previous chill. "But I did think of you. Many times I shared stories of you and me…" He paused. "And my brothers as children. Those moments, for what it may be worth to you, took me momentarily away from the horrors of war."

Those words should be enough and, to a more worthy, honorable woman, they likely would be. Eloise, however, was grasping at all things horrid because selfishly, she wanted more of him.

"What happened to you after I left?" That question seemed dragged out of him, as though he feared an answer, but at the same time, required that piece of her past.

Eloise shifted off his lap and reclaimed the seat opposite him. His mouth tightened. Was it displeasure? Regret? Did a part of him crave her body's nearness the way she craved his? "What you might expect of a young lady," she said with a small shrug. "I went to London. Had a Season. Made a match." Her heart hitched. "My father died shortly after you left." She folded her hands upon her lap and stared at the interlocked digits. The threads holding together the fabric of her life had come undone as neatly as if they'd been plucked and pulled from an embroidery frame.

Lucien leaned across the carriage and rested his hand over hers, comforting, reassuring. She stared at the calluses, rough and coarse. Not at all the hands he'd possessed as a young gentleman. "I am so sorry, Ellie. I should have been there for you."

She managed a smile. "It is fine," she said. At one point it hadn't been. At one time, she'd been empty and aching and alone in her grief. As much as she'd loved and missed her husband and father, life had eventually moved on, taking her with it. Eloise found the courage to continue. "My husband and I returned to London not long after..." Lucien's wife and child had succumbed to their fevers. He gave her a searching look and she amended what she'd intended to say. "He died not even six months after we'd returned to London."

Lucien wiped his hand up and down his cheek then rested it over his lips.

How much loss she'd known.

After he'd returned to find himself a widower, also mourning the loss of his child, he'd languished in a hospital, willing himself to die, contemplating the days and ways in which he could at last end his infernal existence. Yet, Eloise had reentered the world brave and resilient. Admiration built inside him for the woman she'd become. "What was your husband like?" Hopefully the faceless man had been worthy of her.

"Kind," she answered automatically. Good. For if he hadn't been, Lucien would have haunted him in the hereafter. "He was also generous. We became friends and after you'd…"

After he'd left, she'd craved that companionship they'd once known. She didn't need to speak the words.

She colored. "We were friends," she settled for.

An insidious, dark emotion roiled in his gut and threatened to consume him. He balled his hand hard at his side. If he wasn't already bound for hell for the crimes he'd committed against too many in the name of war, he'd be going there now with the envy twisting away at his insides for the man who'd wed her. *Why* should he feel this green snake of jealousy, unless…?

"We didn't have the overwhelming love that clouds all reason and judgment." She shook her head, speaking with a woman's maturity. "But we talked. He cared about my opinions. He listened to me."

She'd deserved that and so much more. So, why did Lucien hate the late earl as he did?

"When most gentlemen treat their wives as property and mere chattel, he entered into a contract that w-would see me…" Her words caught. "That *did* see me cared for." She looked at him, emotion bleeding through her eyes. "He loved me," she said on a shattered whisper. "And he deserved more. The man he was, good, kind, and everything wonderful, he should have known that love." Eloise drew in a ragged breath. "I didn't love him," she whispered those four words, spoken more to herself.

At her admission, some of the pressure eased in Lucien's chest, somehow freeing and terrifying all at the same time.

She dropped her gaze to her tightly clasped hands. "The guilt of that will follow me until I leave this world to join him." She fell into silence. The steady patter of rain upon the carriage roof filled the space. The ping-ping-ping echoing the haunting admission she'd made.

Ah, God. The world was awash in guilt. All these years, he'd lived under the weight of remorse for having failed Sara and his son. That

Eloise should know a like guilt, ripped at him. Lucien leaned across the carriage once more and touched her knee. She lifted her head up. "You can't carry the guilt of that, Ellie," he said quietly. Loyal and loving as she'd been, he'd never known Sherborne, but he'd wager what remained of his black soul that the other man would not want that for her. "You were a good wife to him while he lived. Faithful," he ventured, knowing with the intuitiveness of a person who'd known another soul almost as long as he'd been on this earth that she'd never betrayed her husband.

Her lips twisted in a dry smile. "He may as well have had a dog then."

How did she not see her worth? How could she not realize that whatever years she'd given Sherborne had likely been the happiest the man had ever known? Lucien knew that because some of the most joyous moments in his life had been beside her in the fields of Kent. "Loving you as he did," he murmured, "he would want you to be happy."

Eloise met his gaze square on. "And what of Sara? Would she not want the same for you?"

At her words, he went whipcord straight. He clenched and unclenched his jaw. "It's not the same," he said roughly.

Eloise arched a blonde eyebrow. "Isn't it?" She was relentless. "Do you not carry the same sense of guilt—?"

Lucien raked a hand through his hair. "It is different." Eloise had been there, steadfast and devoted at her husband's side when he'd drawn his last breath. Where had Lucien been? Away, fighting a mad-man because he'd been too weak to gainsay his father's wishes.

She spoke over him. "And her loving you as she did, do you believe she'd want you to have never spoken to your family again? To languish away in a hospital with no one but strangers to care for you—"

"The marchioness is a good woman," he said, his voice increasing in volume. The Marchioness of Drake, with her tenacity, had pulled him back from despair and he would be forever indebted to both her for her kindness and the marquess for his offer of employment.

Eloise scoffed. "Come," she said. "This isn't about the marchioness being a good woman." Help him, she applied the same dogged determination to an argument that she had to spilikens when they'd been mere children. "This is about you being the coward."

Her charge shot through him. "I beg your pardon?" he asked on a silken whisper that would have terrified most men, let alone a mere slip of a woman like Eloise.

Then she'd never been like any other woman he'd known. "A. Coward." She enunciated the two words as clearly as if she schooled someone on a foreign language. "Your father insisted you join the military, your wife died, as did your son," she said with a ruthless pragmatism that made him flinch. "You lost your arm." Eloise ran her otherworldly, blue-green gaze over his face. "And I am so, so sorry that those things happened to you," she said, this time her tone soft. "But they happened, Lucien, and you cannot change them. You cannot change them by pretending your family doesn't exist or by hiding away in the marquess' home as a servant. Not one thing you do will ever restore any of what you lost." She paused. "Except for your family. That is the one matter within your power to heal and fix." Eloise cursed. "If you weren't so damned stubborn to see to it." She sank back in her seat and folded her arms across her heaving chest.

Lucien studied her for a long while. Emotion roiled in his being. Outrage heated the blood in his veins. How callously, how indifferently, she'd tossed those losses he'd suffered in his proverbial face. He wanted to fan the flames of his rage over her calm mention of Sara and his son...and Lucien's arm. Yet, as she held his gaze, her cheeks red from heightened emotion, he couldn't dredge up the suitable fury because, God help him, in their precision, her allegations bore an element of truth.

"Do you have nothing to say?" she cried out.

And because acknowledging Eloise's unerringly accurate charges scared him more than the whole of Boney's army, coward that he was, Lucien did all that he could do to silence her. He reached across the carriage and pulled her onto his lap again.

"What—?"

He kissed her.

SIXTEEN

Eloise stiffened at the unexpectedness of his embrace and then tentatively fisted her hands in the cold, silken tendrils of his thick, black hair, angling his head to better avail herself to him.

He groaned in approval, deepening the kiss. Lucien slid his hand between them and explored her body as if he sought to brand each part of her skin upon his palm. He cupped her breast and then worked the fabric of her décolletage down, exposing her to his gaze. She flushed at the intensity of his eyes trained upon her and made to fold her arms. He halted her movements with a staying hand. "Don't," he ordered gruffly.

She complied and her breath caught with anticipation as he palmed her right breast, weighing it in his hand. Her nipple puckered from his ministrations and he captured the swollen bud between his thumb and forefinger. Eloise bit back a cry, mindful of the impropriety of their actions. "I never..." Her head fell back as he lowered his lips to her breast.

He froze. His breath fanned her exposed skin. "You never what?" he asked on a husky whisper.

"I never knew it could be like this." Every coupling with her husband had been quick, awkward and perfunctory. There had been none of this soul-melting, mind-numbing bliss she knew with Lucien.

He closed his lips over her nipple and a keening moan escaped her lips. Lucien worked the tender bud, worshiping it with his mouth, laving the tip until feeling drove her body alone. Logic ceased to exist. Propriety no longer mattered. Nothing but at last knowing Lucien and...the carriage swayed precariously.

Eloise's stomach lurched. She closed her eyes tightly willing away the queasiness. The driver hit another bump in the road. The contents of her stomach roiled. She scrambled off Lucien's lap and concentrated on breathing once again.

He eyed her through thick, black lashes. A tangible concern replaced the thick haze of desire within his gray depths from moments ago. Lucien ran a searching gaze over her face.

Please do not be sick. Please do not be sick. Please do not be sick. Another bump. She swallowed several times.

An understanding smile tugged at the corners of Lucien's lips.

"It is not amusing," she bit out, those words costing her greatly. She slapped a hand over her mouth and then, by the grace of God, the urge to cast up the contents of her stomach passed.

He shook his head. "I wouldn't dare find humor in your distress, Ellie."

Her heart fluttered.

"I do find your tendency to fall ill in a carriage a rather inconvenient interruption."

Eloise warmed, his meaning clear. She kicked him with the tip of her slipper. "Oh, do hush." He bent and captured her small foot in his hand. She gulped and then the carriage jerked to a stop. Eloise pitched forward, toppling Lucien back and she landed on him in an indignant heap of satin skirts. Eloise scrambled off his lap just as her driver rapped on the carriage door. With quaking fingers, she righted the bodice of her gown.

"We've arrived at an inn, my lady," he shouted into the fierce storm. He opened the door and stinging rain and wind slashed through the entrance.

Lucien leapt down effortlessly, giving no indication that he'd expertly caressed and kissed her until her thoughts jumbled and…

"My lady?"

She gave her head a clearing shake and reached for the driver's hand just as Lucien stepped between them. Eloise accepted his proffered hand and stepped down. Her foot sank into a cold, muddied puddle and she wrinkled her nose, and then quickened her step to match his longer ones. The inn with a crooked wooden sign atop its door beckoned. Lucien shoved the door open and allowed her entry.

The occupants of the full tavern looked as one to the intrusion. A small man, not much taller than her but three times as broad ambled over, little puffs indicating the exertion of his quickened steps. He bowed. "G—"

Lucien spoke, interrupting him. "My lady requires rooms for the evening. Two of them," he hurried to clarify.

The man dabbed at his perspiring brow. "I would gladly provide you rooms."

Splend—

"However, I've but the one, my lord," the innkeeper explained with a regretful smile. He gestured to their sopping frames. "Seems a bit of rain draws the people into a good, comfortable, warm inn." He laughed uproariously, as though he'd told a grand jest.

"You misunderstand the situation," Lucien said. He frowned and surveyed the crowded room of rough-looking men who still eyed them with wariness in their flinty eyes. "Perhaps you might find—"

Eloise jammed her elbow into his side. "My husband," she gave him a pointed look. "And I would welcome the room you do have available."

The man nodded, dislodging the sparse couple of black strands of oily hair slicked over his head. "Very well, my lady." He inclined his head. "If you'll follow me?" He started for the stairs.

Lucien stood stock still. A muscle ticked in the corner of his eye.

She cleared her throat. He was not pleased. Though, the taut set to his broad shoulders and hard glint in his eyes spoke at an emotion a good deal more powerful than displeasure. Fear, desire, and a panicky desperation flared to life within his eyes. "Lucien," she began.

And then with the utterance of his name, all hint of emotion was gone so she wondered if she'd merely willed those emotions into existence.

The innkeeper stopped at the base of the stairs. He shot them a questioning look.

Eloise cast a glance about. "You can't very well sleep in the stables," she said in hushed tones. An embarrassed heat fanned her cheeks at the curious stares they now earned.

"I am not…"

She placed her fingertips on his sleeve and tipped her chin up. "My lord?"

When presented with the possibility of shrugging off Eloise's touch and branding her a liar or allowing her to guide them up the stairs to the lone room in the inn, Lucien erred on the side of the latter.

For all his fury with her interference, her bold lie and the scandal that would be attached to a widow taking a room with the marquess' butler, he'd not see her humiliated. So, he followed. Tension radiated through his being. They'd once been friends. Friends who'd swam together in the frigid lake upon his father's property. They turned down the corridor, following silently behind the innkeeper. He'd merely be sharing close quarters, the same quarters, with the Ellie of his past. The girl with a cheeky smile and tenacious spirit and…

The innkeeper pressed the door handle and motioned them inside.

And now a bed. His gaze fixed on the wide, surprisingly tidy, feathered bed with crisp, white linens and a floral coverlet.

Eloise removed her hand from his sleeve and entered the chambers. She walked a small circle about the room, taking it in silently. Then, she favored the innkeeper with a smile. "Thank you, Mr…?"

"Rooney," he supplied quickly. His cheeks turned pink and he eyed her with a mooncalf expression.

"Mr. Rooney." She widened her smile. "Thank you for your assistance."

Did the older man sigh?

Lucien balled his hand into a fist, detesting her impact on men. When did little Eloise learn to smile like…like…that? As though a man was the only one in the room. A seductive smile that reminded him very clearly that she might still possess the cheeky smile and tenacious spirit but was no longer a girl. Had one of those scoundrels vying for a place in her bed schooled her on such lessons? "That will be all," he snapped.

Mr. Rooney jumped and, with an incoherent mutter, tripped over his own feet in his haste to take his leave.

Eloise's smile faded and it was like a cloud had blotted out the sun. "I do not like this side of you, Lucien," she said, as though she were scolding a child.

He took a step toward her. "And which side is that, Eloise?" he said on a lethal whisper.

She retreated. "The angry one." She slashed the air with a hand. "The gentleman who now speaks like…like…"

He advanced. "Like what?"

"Like a man who was not raised as though he's a viscount's son."

Lucien paused before her. Their knees brushed. "And it matters so much to you that I'm no longer that viscount's son?"

Eloise craned her head back to look at him. "You will always be the viscount's son. You may take on the position of stable hand, footman, or butler but you will always be a gentleman."

He wanted to spit scathing words at her. Taunt her for daring to believe he could ever be Mr. Lucien Jonas, the third son of an affluent viscount. End whatever foolish pull that existed between them.

Only…he took a step away. He turned and stared blankly at the window. For five years, the ultimate revenge, the only revenge, he'd had against his father, insistent on that commission, was Lucien's rejection of his family. He'd returned from war and turned his back on his family, his lineage, and the role of gentleman. Not realizing until this very moment with Eloise's words that his was a hollow victory. The work he'd taken on, though honorable and sure to infuriate his father, would never bring Sara back.

Lucien called forth her face. He squeezed his eyes tight and tried to draw in an image he'd carried in his heart and mind for almost six years, a visage that wouldn't come. Instead, tightly coiled, blonde curls, a blue-green stare, and a slender frame flooded his mind.

Eloise touched his shoulder.

He jumped. His heart thumped hard and fast in his chest as panic besieged his senses.

"What is it, Lucien?" Her husky voice wrapped around those four words.

Lucien shook his head and started for the door.

A rustle of skirts and the soft shuffle of slippered feet filled the quiet space. Eloise placed herself between him and the door, blocking his escape. "No." He took a step right. She matched his step. "I said no. You don't simply get to run away." Again.

"Is that what you believe I've done?"

She arched an eyebrow. "Isn't it?"

"You don't know a bloody thing about it." He strode around her.

"For someone who is a friend, you certainly have a low opinion of me," she called out, staying his hand. "You consider me weak. You believe I don't know the first thing to Sunday about struggle. You believe I haven't faced tragedy and why?" Her voice hitched. "Because I didn't go off to fight a war, Lucien? I lost, too, in life."

Her words had the same effect as a lance being driven through his heart and the muscles of his stomach contracted under the weight of her admission. She spoke, clearly interpreting his tense silence for condemnation. "But if I allow myself to dwell on the unfairness of it all, it would drown me and I deserve more."

She did. She deserved so much more.

"And you deserve more, too," she finished, her words so faint he strained to hear.

Lucien focused on the ping of rain slapping the leaded window-pane and the creak of the floorboards as Eloise shifted on her feet. Those innocuous sounds prevented him from thinking about his own loss, but on everything she'd suffered, all the loss she'd known. Agony turned in his belly and he nearly cracked under the weight of that pain. The girl Eloise had been and the woman she'd become deserved more than a tragic, empty, lonely existence. That fate was reserved for cold-hearted bastards who did things in the name of battle and were consigned to hell for those sins—men like Lucien and so many others. But not Ellie. Ellie was good and pure and worthy in ways he never would be.

"I have to go," he said, his voice hoarse. Without a backward glance, he left.

SEVENTEEN

Eloise stared at the untouched tray of food brought up earlier that evening by a pretty, blonde serving woman. Not her *husband.* Or at least her pretend husband, anyway.

No, Lucien had hightailed it out of their room and disappeared. The moments had ticked by. The storm eventually broke with the faintest traces of sunlight slanting through the gray, storm clouds. Eventually, the night sky drove back all hint of day...and he still did not come.

She lay down and looked up at the plaster ceiling. Faint chips marred the paint. With a sigh, Eloise flung her forearm over her brow, blotting out her view of the depressing ceiling. And why should he return? One, she was not his wife and he protected both his position with the marquess and her reputation lest he share her room and word of that reached others. Two, he resented her for interfering in his familial relationships. She turned onto her side and stared out at the night sky. Three, he no longer liked her. Her lips twisted. Oh, he liked her enough to kiss her to silence as he was now wont to do, but a kiss borne of annoyance was not love. It wasn't even a polite regard.

Eloise chewed at her lower lip. And he would like her a good deal less if he discovered she'd failed Sara. What would he think of Eloise then?

Lucien was a man who loved with a grand depth but was also given to other emotions with a like intensity. The antipathy he carried for his father, the resentment he bore for his brothers, her...She swallowed past a ball of emotion clogging her throat. It was an inevitability.

He'd ultimately learn the truth and Lucien, that man of great passions, would never be able to separate her from that heartbreaking loss he'd suffered.

Eloise would slice off her littlest fingers if she could have him see her as more than little Ellie Gage. But in having spent those final, sorrowful days with the one and only woman who would ever truly hold his heart, nothing more could ever come of her and Lucien. And likely now, not even a friendship. In her, he would forever see the woman who failed to save his wife and child, and be forever reminded of that loss.

Eloise blinked back the useless tears that blurred her vision. She grabbed the coverlet and dabbed at the corners of her eyes where the blasted drops had squeezed out.

The click of the door handle blared like the flare of a pistol. She froze. The door closed once more and then the click of a lock. In the time she'd spent with Lucien since she'd found him in London, she'd already come to identity the stealthy, graceful steps of one so tall. He strode over to the bed and she pressed her eyes closed feigning sleep. She drew in slow, even breaths.

Lucien froze at the edge of the bed and remained rooted to the spot. He stood so long that Eloise's body ached from holding herself immobile under his scrutiny. She remembered to maintain a slow, even cadence of her breathing. Seconds? Minutes? Hours later, the floor creaked in protest as he lay down. Eloise stared unblinking at the opposite side of the wall. He'd come.

Granted, he intended to sleep on the cold floor without a blanket or pillow and—

"I know you aren't asleep, Ellie."

She jumped. Without a word, she grabbed the pillow beside her and dropped it over the edge of the bed, hitting him in the face. "Oomph." She heaved the coverlet over the side of the bed. It landed with a thump on his chest.

"You're angry with me."

Eloise screwed up her mouth. She was angry that he was angry; at life, his family, her. She grabbed her own pillow and dropped it on his head.

He sighed.

She flipped back over onto her side, knowing she was being a petulant child, and really wished she hadn't given over her own pillow as well. The lout.

Lucien tossed the white, feathered pillow back onto the bed. It hit her in the cheek and bounced several inches, nearly falling off the bed. "Would you care to talk of it?"

Now? *Now* he'd speak of it? She bit the inside of her cheek to keep from reminding him that he'd dashed off, *also* like a petulant child. "There is nothing to say," she said automatically.

"Would you have me ruin your reputation?" he shot back. His tone hinted at annoyance over her dismissal.

Eloise flipped back onto her side and leaned over the side of the bed. "I'm a world-wary widow, Lucien. I can't be ruined."

"You know that's not true," he said, shoving himself up onto his elbow. "You're susceptible to gossip, my lady."

Her gaze was involuntarily drawn to the empty space his arm had once been. Odd, he moved with such grace, elegance, and confidence that she often forgot he'd lost one of those precious limbs. Eloise sat up. She drew her knees close to her chest and folded her arms about her legs. "I have loved you longer than I remember, Lucien, and yet, for all the years I've known you, you've always infuriated me. You are stubborn and obstinate—"

"They mean the same thing," he pointed out unnecessarily.

"But you never pushed anyone away, until you returned..." *From the war.* She let the thought go unfinished. She knew nothing of war or what men were forced to do or be on those battlefields but imagined those experiences were indelibly burned on each soldier's memory. "Until you returned," she repeated softly, to herself. Perhaps the demons he now hid from were not her, the viscount, his brothers, not even Sara. Perhaps he hid from the life he'd lived while away from them all. She rubbed her chin back and forth over the tops of her knees. "Have you missed them?"

He sat up and mimicked her pose, drawing his knees against his chest. "Them?"

Eloise pointed her eyes at the ceiling. "Do not pretend to misunderstand." She inched closer to the side of the bed. "Your brothers." She took care to omit mention of his father. "They've thought of you often."

"Have they?" he inquired, his tone non-committal.

"There's not been a time I've seen them when they've not mentioned your name."

The darkening of his eyes, however, indicated anything but regard for his loving, loyal brothers. "You've seen them often?" he asked gruffly.

She nodded. "They were there when I made my Come Out." She slid her gaze away. "And when my father died and then my husband." They'd also been there to see her cared for after she'd fallen ill tending to Sara and his son. The finest physician had been sent at the viscount's bequest, the original family doctor sacked after Sara succumbed to fever.

"I'm sorry." His voice, still scratchy as if from ill use, penetrated her thoughts.

She lifted her shoulders in a little shrug. "It's—"

Lucien stood and claimed a spot on the edge of the bed. The feather mattress dipped under his weight. "For not being there," he said. "I should have been there."

Their legs brushed and she glanced down at his thick, well-muscled leg pressed against her more delicate one. How very different this powerful, imposing man was than the boy of her youth. "Yes," she whispered. "You should have been there." Suddenly those words, a freeing admission gave her strength. "I do not begrudge you for loving Sara. But I was a friend to you and you simply forgot me." His skin turned an ashen gray, but she'd not allow guilt to stifle the flow of her words. "I needed you, Lucien. You were my friend…and you would have chosen death over me?" If it hadn't been for the marchioness, he would have. Eloise would be forever indebted to the other woman, but she'd always be hurt that she herself had meant so little to him.

He caressed her cheek. "There are far too many things in my life I've done that I'm not proud of." Lucien ran his gaze over her face. "But having turned away from you, when you needed me, that has to

116

be one of my greatest offenses." He brushed his thumb over her lower lip, that simple touch scorching.

And knowing these handful of days would be the last she ever had with him, Eloise leaned up and kissed him.

He should pull back. He should turn his head, stride over to the door, yank it open, and find his sleep in the stables. There were a number of things Lucien should have done. Now…and in his miserable life on the whole.

However, he'd developed an abysmal habit of doing the opposite of what he should.

So, he kissed Eloise. Kissed her because the four kisses he'd known before this moment were not enough, nor would they ever be enough. He cupped his hand about the graceful arch of her neck so he could better avail himself to her mouth. She opened in invitation and he slid his tongue inside. Eloise moaned and he reveled in the sweet, vibrating hum of her desire. Lucien shifted his hand down, guided it about her waist, and lowered her down upon the soft, feather mattress.

"So beautiful," he whispered, trailing kisses from the corner of her lips, down her neck, and lower to the gape in her nightgown. *Push me away.*

Eloise wrapped her hands about his neck, anchoring him in place. "Please don't stop." Her entreaty came out as a whispery moan, knowing his thoughts because this was Ellie and she'd always known what he was thinking, even when he himself did not. "I've spent my whole life loving you, Lucien. I want all of you."

There would be time enough for regrets and reasons and logic in the morn. For now, there was just the two of them. As he slipped off her modest robe and tugged her nightshift over her head, Lucien committed himself to memorizing every last inch of Eloise. He cupped her breast and raised it to his mouth.

A sweet sigh escaped her as he closed his lips over the peak of her breast. He sucked and laved the engorged, pink tip until her breath grew rapid and her legs fell open in an invitation. He drew back and shrugged out of his jacket. His hand went to his breeches and he paused. With that prolonged stretch, he willed her to be the lone person of reason in this moment of madness.

Eloise pushed herself up. "Here," she murmured, her voice husky with desire. She worked his breeches off. He kicked them aside.

A groan slipped past his lips as her clever fingers found his throbbing shaft. Eloise fisted him and tugged gently. "You will be the death of me," he said on an agonized whisper.

"I certainly hope not." Her words ended on a moan as he guided her back down once more. He braced himself on his side and ran his hand down her body, his fingers seeking out her hot center, pausing at the thatch of golden curls. For a moment, reality reared its vicious head reminding him the woman he made love to was, in fact, Ellie Gage, now a countess and he a mere butler. Two people who could never share more than a past...

She splayed her legs and bit her lip. "Please," she begged.

And he was lost. Lucien slipped a finger inside and found her passage slick with desire. She cried out and clenched her legs about his hand, encouraging him. He played with the slick, swollen nub at her center until keening, senseless moans of desire blended with her pleading cries for surcease.

Lucien shifted his weight above her and parted her legs with his knee. Sweat dotted his forehead. A lone bead dripped into his eyes, blinding and he blinked. He'd have gladly traded his vision for the glory of this moment. He guided his shaft to the apex of her thighs and then went still. Lucien took in Eloise's flushed cheeks and swollen lips.

Take her. You are two adults who know your bodies and minds. A pressure tightened inside his chest.

I cannot. For all the ways in which he'd neglected Eloise as a friend through the years, he could not simply make hard and fast love to her. Could not, when she, as a lady and as a loyal woman, deserved more than a quick coupling with a man who'd never been worthy of her. If he did this, he would be no different than those roguish bastards who'd vied for a place in the young widow's bed.

Now knowing the same effort called forth by that Titan God, Atlas, with those celestial spheres, Lucien drew back, the agony of his decision a near physical pain. He rolled away from her and stared at the dreary paint-chipped ceiling. His breath came harsh and fast, blending with Eloise's rapid gasps.

The mattress dipped as she came up on her knees beside him. "Why…what…?" She ran her passion-clouded eyes frantically over his face, as if she searched for answers to account for his abrupt withdrawal.

He flung his forearm over his eyes. "I'm s—"

Eloise yanked his arm back with a stunning force. "Don't you do that." She glared. Her eyes, previously heavy with desire, now flashed rage. "I don't want your apologies. I'm a woman, who knows my mind."

"You are a lady."

She jutted her chin out. "I am a widow."

Lucien sat up and flung his legs over the side of the bed. He captured her chin between his thumb and forefinger. "But you're still a lady." And he'd not disrespect her by taking her outside the bonds of matrimony. He imagined a wedded state with her. A small girl born to them with impossibly thick, tight, blonde curls. Marriage to *Ellie*? He choked on his swallow. Surely he could not, would not, ever dare consider marriage to Eloise. She was his friend. Then this desire for her defied all bonds of friendship.

With his mind in tumult, Eloise shrugged off his touch. "You remember so easily that I'm a lady." She held his gaze. "Yet so casually forget that you are, in fact, a gentleman."

No matter how many posts he accepted with the marquess, or the distinction between them now…he had been born a gentleman. Whether he wished it or not.

Lucien stood. He suspected if he stole one more glance at Eloise, in her naked glory, fire in her aquamarine eyes, he would gladly abandon the life he'd established for himself these past two years. With swift movements, he collected his clothes and quickly pulled them on. When fully clothed, he strode over to the door. And for the second time that night, left her.

EIGHTEEN

They departed the following morning. Eloise stepped out of the inn and held her hand over her eyes to shield them from the blindingly bright morning glare. What had once seemed a miserable and dark journey was now filled with glorious hope. She sucked in a deep breath, allowing the clean, country air to cleanse her lungs.

"Are you ready, my lady?"

Lucien's cool, perfunctory words slashed into her momentary giddiness. She glanced at him. The tender, gentle lover of the previous evening was gone. In his place was the unsmiling, unyielding Lucien Jones, returned soldier. She favored him with a frown.

Alas, he appeared immune to her displeasure. He tipped his head pointedly toward the carriage. With a toss of her curls, Eloise strode down the cobbled path. She picked her way over the muddied puddles. How could he be so indifferent after what had transpired last evening?

Because nothing transpired, you silly fool. Eloise's slipper caught the edge of a cobbled stone and she stumbled.

Lucien settled his arm about her waist, steadying her. She stole an upward glance at him. "Thank you," she murmured.

He gave a brusque nod, his mouth tense.

They reached the carriage and the driver pulled the door open. He held a hand out to assist her up. She hesitated a moment and stole a peak at Lucien. However, he withdrew, fading back a step. A servant once more. Damn him.

She climbed into the carriage with Mr. Nell's help. He closed the door behind her. Furrowing her brow, Eloise tugged aside the velvet curtain. A servant rushed forward with Lucien's mount. Of course he wouldn't join her. Humiliated shame dug at her insides. He found her company so objectionable he didn't want to share the same carriage.

Feeling her gaze, Lucien looked over at her. She let the curtain go and it fluttered into place. Eloise sat in pained embarrassment at being caught studying him when he should be so very indifferent to her.

The carriage lurched forward and so with the forward movement went her stomach. She lowered her head on the comfortable plush squabs of the well-sprung carriage. For the first time in every single miserable carriage ride she'd taken in her twenty-eight years, she gave thanks for the distraction. Her stomach churned. Even if it was a miserable distraction.

The misery of her roiling belly was vastly preferable to the toe-curling shame of Lucien's rejection. She groaned and it had nothing to with the jarring bump of the carriage steadily increasing in speed. Instead, it had everything to do with reliving that humiliating moment of Lucien effortlessly setting her away when her body had ached with the pleasure only he could show her.

Eloise slapped her hands over her face and shook her head back and forth. "You are a fool," she whispered, the words muffled by her hands. The sooner she realized there never was, nor ever would be, anything with Lucien, the sooner she could go back to living her life.

But how could she? How, when he was so very real again? If even a jaded, coarser version of his younger self?

She closed her eyes and sought the blessed oblivion of sleep, welcoming the edge of unconsciousness that drew her in.

The carriage hit a jarring bump. Her eyes flew open as she careened into the side of the carriage. "Oomph." Eloise winced and shoved away from the wall. She rubbed her forearm and yawned, her muddled mind trying to sort through her whereabouts. Then the conveyance drew to a hard, jerky halt.

"Bloody hell man, have a care!" Lucien's thunderous shout penetrated her confusion and with it reminded her of the purpose of her journey, their journey, and his rejection.

She groaned...

Just as Lucien wrenched the carriage door open. He did an up and down search of her. "Are you hurt?"

"N—"

The thought went unfinished as he wrapped his arm around her waist and guided her out of the carriage.

Mr. Nell leapt from atop his perch with surprising agility for one so portly. "Many pardons, my lady," he said. He plucked his cap from his head and dusted it against his leg. "The roads are muddied from the storms and you'd indicated you wanted to make the journey as quickly as possible."

She opened her mouth.

"Not at the expense of the lady's life," Lucien seethed.

Mr. Nell's skin turned waxen and he stumbled back at the ferocious glower trained on him.

Eloise inserted herself between the scowling Lucien and her driver. "That will be all, Mr. Nell," she said with a gentle smile. He slapped his black cap upon his baldpate and, with a deep bow, reclaimed his seat atop the box. Eloise shifted her attention to Lucien. "You do not need to be a beast to him," she said chidingly.

He continued to glare over her head at the servant. Mr. Nell, however, was wise enough to direct his focus out at the sprawling, green pastures. "You could be killed for his recklessness."

Perhaps Lucien did not understand the magnitude of his father's grave situation. "I asked he set a rigorous pace." Removed as he was these many years, he failed to realize that the once proud, bold viscount was at the final moments of his life.

He made a sound of impatience. "Very well, then you'd be killed for your recklessness."

She laughed. "You are insufferable."

Lucien managed a reluctant smile. The right corner of his lips tugged up slowly, the left following suit in a rusty display of amusement.

Her laughter died. How many times had he found joy over the years? She ventured very few. A gentle, spring breeze stirred her skirts and displaced a single curl. It fell over her eye.

They moved in unison. Lucien shot his hand out just as she made to brush the strand back. Their hands connected and the thrilling shock of his touch coursed through her. She wanted it to mean nothing. Wanted to adopt the affected indifference of a bold, experienced widow who'd not be so shamed by the rejection she had suffered last evening.

But then, he raised the single tress. He rubbed it between his thumb and forefinger, transfixed by the lock. She could never feign indifference where Lucien was concerned. With slow, reluctant movements, he released the strand and took a step back. "We should leave," he said quietly.

Eloise glanced up at the sun wondering how long she'd slept. "Yes." There were likely several more hours of travel.

Lucien tugged his timepiece out. "It is nearly two o'clock. We should arrive within two hours." He gave another crooked grin. "Or fewer considering your driver's recklessness." It took a moment for his jesting words to register. Instead, she stared at the gold timepiece, a gift given him by his father when he'd been a boy of sixteen. Her heart hitched. A man who truly abhorred his father would not hold onto a material possession that would forever remind him of his parent.

He followed her gaze. The sun reflected off the gleaming gold. "You kept it," she said. She expected the angry man he'd become would stuff the piece into his pocket and dismiss her observation.

Lucien studied the gold piece, cradling it in his palm. He nodded and walked off to the edge of the road.

Eloise shifted on her feet and stared after him, silent and contemplative. His head remained bent over the gift given him by the viscount. Periodically, he'd look up at the vibrant poppies blanketing the fields, a crimson explosion of color, so vast it dominated the landscape.

He looked at her. "I didn't come," he said.

She cocked her head and stared at him questioningly.

Lucien turned silently to the sea of poppies. He stuffed his hand into his pocket, the gesture so reminiscent of young Lucien, her heart ached with the remembrance. Only this man, broad, powerful, missing part of his arm, and more, the hope in his heart bore no other traces to the innocent youth he'd been.

Eloise wandered over, the patiently waiting driver forgotten. She stood at Lucien's side and stared out at the scenescape.

"I had promised to meet you," he said, his voice rough with unchecked emotion. "And I didn't come."

She caught her lower lip between her teeth and gave a jerky shake of her head. "No. You didn't."

That had been the day he'd met the new vicar's daughter…and the day Eloise had ceased to matter.

He turned to her. He ran an emotion-laden stare over her face. "You mattered, Ellie."

She tried to force a smile that wouldn't come.

"You did," he insisted, his tone harsh. He reached for her and then glanced over her head at the waiting carriage bearing the servant and trunks. "You always mattered," he said in hushed undertones.

Eloise turned her face up to the sun and welcomed the soothing caress of the warm rays upon her cheeks. "Of course I did," she said, because she'd always believed she mattered to him. "I merely ceased to matter in the way I once did."

A denial sprung fast and hard to Lucien's lips. The bond he'd shared with Eloise had oftentimes defied the closeness he'd known even with his brothers. Oft regarded as the young, underfoot brother, Eloise had thrust him into the role of escapade-leader. He would lead them on their merry scrapes and she would follow. Then, he had simply set aside the closeness between them, for his love of Sara. A powerful, instantaneous love of a young man who'd seen a glorious beauty he could not live without.

He stole a long, sideways look at Eloise, her face tilted to the sun, her cheeks pink from the warmth of the day. And the love he'd had for her had been of friend, confidante…and he'd forgotten her. God help him. "I'm so sorry, Eloise," he said.

Her eyes flew open. She looked at him questioningly.

The worst part of life, he'd discovered, had not been in the mistakes he'd made, but rather in his inability to go back and undo each of them, and put his life and the lives of those he'd loved to rights. He gestured to the fields. "I was to meet you—"

"It was silly—"

"In the fields of poppies to pick the blooms and I—"

She lifted her shoulders in a nonchalant shrug, the casual gesture only belied by the hurt in her tone. "Why, would you? You were a man of nineteen. I was just barely a woman at seventeen." Eloise folded her arms across her chest, as though hugging herself. "That was the day you met Sara."

She remembered that pivotal moment in his life. Remembered because she had always been more of a friend to him than he'd ever been to her and he'd left her standing in a field of wildflowers. Even if the woman who'd ensnared his attention that day would go on to be his wife, forgetting Eloise as he had, was unpardonable.

He stepped forward and waded into the sea of red blooms.

Eloise called out after him. "Where…?"

He spun slowly around and held out his hand, motioning her forward. "These are here now."

Eloise of old would have danced merrily into the flowers, spun in circles until she was dizzy with the scent of spring. The cautious woman who'd also known great loss looked hesitantly at the carriage. She returned her attention to him, with a slight frown. "Lucien, we do not have time—"

"We've already lost too many moments, Eloise. Let us have this one."

She hesitated and lifted her skirts. Her slipper hovered above the earth.

"Both of us have been surrounded by so much death." Too much. Countless, faceless men. His wife. Child. Her husband. Her father. His father would soon be gone.

Eloise shook her head. "We cannot escape." They could not escape death. Her meaning was clearer than had she spoken that omitted word.

"No." He inclined his head. "But we might steal a moment of happiness where we can."

And with that, Eloise completed that step. She loosened the strings of her bonnet and shoved the piece back and then walked over to him. She moved with more graceful, practiced steps, a woman's steps that carried her over to him. She stopped. "Well?" she asked, arching an eyebrow.

He flicked the tip of her nose the way he'd done when she'd been a vexing girl. "Never tell me you've forgotten how to pick flowers."

Eloise swatted his arm. "You're as incorrigible as ever." Her laughter rang clear as tinkling bells through the rolling fields.

Lucien angled his head down, awkwardly motioning to his half-empty sleeve. "I may require some assistance, my lady. I fear my flower picking abilities are not once what they'd been."

She snorted. "Oh, hush. You require about as much help as you did then, which is none at all." With that, the tension, pain, and regret of their pasts melted away and she flitted through the field, an emerald splash of green muslin amidst the fields of poppies. Eloise stooped and picked a single bloom. "Here." She held it up.

Lucien stood in silence, accepting the selected buds she handed off to him. For so long, bitter resentment had burned like a poison inside him. He'd accepted the black mark upon his soul was to be a penance for the acts he'd committed against other men in the name of his country...and for abandoning his wife and child. Now, staring at her, time frozen in this field of flowers, he was stricken by the realization that he was...for the first time...in five years—happy. He braced for the flood of guilt. Where were the sentiments of remorse and that sense of unworthiness which had followed him all these years?

Instead, a lightness filled his chest at that freeing acknowledgement.

"Splendid!" Eloise brushed her gloved hands upon the front of her skirts and stood. "We shall give them to your father." With a smile she took the makeshift bouquet from him. "Granted, they'll likely be all wilted by then," she prattled on with the same youthful exuberance she'd exhibited as a girl plucking flowers from a field. "Here." She withdrew a single bloom and tucked it into the front pocket of his jacket. "This one shall be for you." Her smile widened. "Shall we?"

With that, she started back for the carriage, not pausing to see if he followed her questioning words.

Likely because she already knew that just then, he would follow her anywhere. Lucien stood transfixed by the seductive sway of her hips. Just then a gleam of sun lit upon the crown of her head and turned those blonde tresses to spun gold. Ah God, how he wanted her. Through her resolve, courage, and strength, Eloise, with an effortless ease, managed something Boney and all his men had failed to do. She'd marched over his heart and laid siege to the organ he'd thought dead.

Perhaps not all surrenders were altogether bad. With a grin on his lips, he started after her.

NINETEEN

One hour, fifty-six minutes and a handful of seconds later, they arrived at Lucien's childhood home. He tucked his timepiece back in his pocket and dismounted from his horse.

A servant rushed forward to accept his horse. The young man, likely no older than twenty years or so, was unfamiliar to him. How many other unfamiliar faces would he find? With reluctance, he took in the impressive stone facade of the structure he'd called home. Regal and elegant with wide, stone steps and floor-length windows along the front of the façade, his skin prickled with a sense of being studied from someone behind one of those windows.

Absorbed as he was, a man stepping back into his past, he started when Eloise sidled up to him. "Forgive me," he murmured. "I…"

"It's all right," she said. She slipped her hands into his hand and gave a faint squeeze.

His throat worked. For his insistence that she remain behind in London, he found himself suddenly very grateful for her presence here. These handful of days they'd spent together melded his past and present, and he who'd prided himself on needing no one these past years, found himself needing…her. "Ellie," he said, his voice came out garbled under the weight of his discovery.

He loved her. Loved her for who she'd been and the friendship they'd shared but more, he loved her for the woman she was—a bold, defiant, determined lady who refused to let him to dwell in the resentment and anger and bitterness of his past.

She angled her head. "Lucien—"

The front door opened and, as one, they swung their gazes to the door. Two men filed out the entranceway. A slender golden haired lady with spectacles perched on the edge of her nose hovered in the entranceway staring curiously down at him. This must be Palmer's wife. His brother had married several years back. Two? Mayhap three years ago?

His brothers now conversed with Eloise, nodding periodically at whatever questions she put to them. He felt the worst sort of interloper on a familial tableau he didn't belong in. Lucien took a step back. But for Eloise, Richard and Palmer had been his best friends through the years. Time had turned them into older, more mature figures he barely recognized. In Palmer's case, a wedded gentleman to a woman Lucien had never even met.

Richard claimed her hands and raised them to his lips one at a time. "Ellie," he said with such familiarity that a stone pitted in Lucien's stomach.

"Richard," she said, smiling up at him with that smile Lucien had believed was reserved for him.

You were gone, a voice needled.

The tendrils of jealousy fanned out and spread through every corner of his being as he stood, an interloper on the intimate exchange between Eloise and his brothers. He'd not considered the possibility that his Ellie could be, that she might be, something more to either of his brothers. Seeing the way they spoke with smiles and grins and her soft blushes, he confronted the truth—their lives together had continued without him. Lucien had left. First for war and then in his choosing to cut himself apart from his family and, in that time, the friendship they three had known, continued.

It was wrong for this seething envy to eat away at him like a poison. With Richard and Palmer's intact bodies, refined manners, and easy smiles, the glaring differences between him and his brothers shone, never more obvious than in this moment. Richard would make her a far better husband. Lucien had nothing to offer her. He retreated a step. He'd been foolish to come. He didn't want this life. Didn't want…

Richard said something that drove back Eloise's smile. She gave a slight nod and then stepped aside and with that movement, she provided his brothers an unfettered view of Lucien.

The tension between them fairly crackled with a lifelike quality. Palmer and Richard stared with eyes, a shade of gray that may as well have been his own, at Lucien's empty sleeve, to the place his arm should be. He clenched and unclenched his jaw, detesting the idea that he should be an object of pity to them.

Lucien jutted out his jaw and then wordlessly, held out his hand.

Richard studied it a while, as though he'd never before seen five fingers and then took it. He yanked Lucien into his arms. "Lucien," he said, folding him in a grip hard enough to raise bruises.

He stiffened but then blinked as emotion rolled through him. A feeling of coming home.

"I've missed you," Richard said, his voice harsh with emotion and then cleared his throat. The dull flush on his cheeks hinted at embarrassment over his lack of restraint. He stepped away and Palmer, the heir to the viscountcy, stepped forward.

Broader than he remembered with more harsh, angular planes to his face, he evinced the same aura of power and strength as their father. "Lucien," his baritone so very similar to Father's that it may as well have been the viscount greeting his son.

Lucien tried to force the words out, but he'd been solitary for so long he couldn't form them. "I…"

Richard slapped him on the back. "I know," he said, sparing him from exposing his soul to them on the front steps of their childhood home with curious servants as their witnesses.

Lucien turned to Eloise just as Richard held out his arm. She placed her fingertips upon his expensive, sapphire coat sleeve, and the cost of that garment greater than all the clothes he'd donned as a patient at London Hospital or servant combined. He curled his hand so tight he dug crescent marks upon his palm.

Eloise cast a lingering glance back at him and then returned her attention to Richard. Lucien stared after them until they'd disappeared inside. He registered Palmer's knowing stare. "So, you've at last

130

noticed, Ellie," he said with a small grin. And just like that, the years melted away and it was as though he'd never left.

"Leave off," Lucien growled and then took the steps two at a time after them. His brother's amused chuckle trailed after him. He drew to a slow, uncertain stop at the slip of a young woman. Poised at the entrance, she stood almost as a sentry between Lucien and the hallowed walls of his youth.

His sister-in-law. Under the intensity of his scrutiny, she smoothed her hands over the front of her skirts. "Hullo," she murmured, stepping outside.

Palmer came over and settled a palm at her waist. "I'd introduce you to my wife, Julianne," he said. "Julianne, this is my brother." His words broke.

Lucien bowed his head. "How do you do?" he asked, once again shamed that he'd so easily shut his brothers from his life. He didn't know how the young couple had met. Whether theirs had been a love match. How much he'd missed.

Julianne gave him a tentative smile. "It is a pleasure." She looked to her husband and a pretty blush suffused her cheeks. "I have heard so many stories of you and I am so very glad you've come."

Palmer saved him from searching for a suitable reply. He placed a hand upon his shoulder. "Father is ill." All earlier levity, replaced by the somber, cautioning tone.

Tears flooded Julianne's pale blue eyes.

Lucien nodded. "I—"

"No." Palmer shook his head. "I…" He swiped a hand over his mouth. "You'll not recognize him," he said. "He's been asking for you."

Lucien squared his jaw, but none of the previous seething hatred he felt for the viscount came. Filled with a sudden disquiet at his brother's ominous admission, he stepped through the front doors. The housekeeper was still the same plump, red-cheeked woman he remembered from his youth. Only streaks of white painted her chestnut brown hair. Mrs. Flora said something to Eloise.

A spasm of grief contorted Eloise's face and she took the housekeeper's hands in hers and gave a squeeze. Tears filled the loyal servant's eyes and she nodded. Eloise released her and the woman discreetly dabbed at her eyes. She turned to him and then her eyes widened like a night owl startled from its perch. "Master Lucien," she cried and then the tears fell freely down her cheeks.

Lucien went taut. Years of fighting had stolen the luxury of unrestrained emotion from him. To exhibit even a hint of weakness meant death. He'd lived by that code and more, he'd lived away from loved ones so long he forgot to move about them. "Mrs. Flora," he said gruffly.

"It is so very good to see you." She looked to Richard. "The viscount will be…" her voice broke. "Happy."

Richard rested a hand upon his shoulder. "The doctor just left his side a short while ago, Lucien." Emotion burned strong in the other man's eyes. "I do not know how much longer he shall live."

One week ago, before Eloise had slipped back into his life and stolen into his heart restoring his spirit, Lucien would have had a vastly different reaction to that pronouncement. He'd have sneered and said the viscount could burn in hell and not given his sire another thought. Now, taking in the swell of emotion in his brothers' and Eloise's solemn expressions, the magnitude of this loss rocked him.

"We should see him now." *If you intend to.* The implication as loud as if it had been spoken.

Lucien nodded jerkily and fell into step beside his brother. He made it to the middle of the sweeping, marble staircase and registered Eloise at the base, standing beside Palmer and Julianne. He turned to her expectantly. "Will you come with me?" He needed her to be there. He'd feigned indifference for five years. She'd forced him to confront the truth of his lie.

"Of course," she said simply. Eloise climbed the stairs. Her gown wrinkled from a long day's travel, the hem of her skirt muddied from their traipsing through the poppies. She trailed along behind him as they wound their way down the corridor. How many other ladies would have put aside their own material comforts to join a surly bastard such as Lucien to visit a dying man?

He staggered a step and his brother's gaze registered a question. Lucien quickly righted himself and continued his forward stride. Ah, he'd been so very indifferent. He'd spent years hating his father, begrudging him for the commission that had sent him off to war. Now he realized that it had been easier to place blame, hating his father, than to confront the lack of control Lucien had over any aspect of his life—his sanity, his wife and child's well-being, hell he couldn't have even protected his own bloody arm.

They stopped before the viscount's chambers. Lucien's palm grew damp and he dusted it along the side of his wrinkled pants.

Eloise captured it in her small, capable hands. He fixed his gaze on their interlocked digits for a moment. She gave him a gentle smile and squeezed his fingers, her touch comforting and yet capable for one so small. Then she released him.

His brother pressed the door handle and motioned him inside.

Lucien stepped into the darkened chambers. He froze as the door closed quietly behind him with a soft, decisive click. In spite of the warm day, a fire blazed in the hearth, the curtains remained closely tightened blotting out all hint of light. His eyes struggled to adjust to the dimly lit room and then he located the small figure at the center of the massive four-poster bed. A pressure tightened about his lungs, making it difficult to draw breath. He strode over to the bed.

His throat closed painfully and he swallowed hard. The emaciated figure, with his gaunt face, bore no hint of resemblance to the commanding, powerful viscount. His father slumbered, drawing in an occasional, ragged breath. He cleared his throat. What a waste. What a goddamn waste his hatred had been. And for what? What had any of it gotten him? It hadn't brought Sara or his son back. It hadn't even brought him a small measure of satisfaction.

Lucien took a slow breath and searched about for a seat. He pulled the King Louis XIV chair closer to the bed. The mahogany legs scraped along the hard wood of the floor.

His father struggled to open his eyes. "R-Richard," his voice emerged a hollow croak.

133

He closed his eyes a moment. "N-no, Father," he said, his voice breaking. "It is Lucien."

The dying man stilled and then blinked his bloodshot eyes. "L-Lucien?" He shoved himself up onto his elbows.

Lucien rested a staying hand upon his shoulder. "Don't, Father."

Tears flooded his eyes. "Ah, God, Lucien…" A tear streaked down his cheek. "I-I have missed you my boy."

The sight of that single drop from a man who'd represented power and strength, who'd possessed an indomitable spirit that could not be shaken, that one lone tear a final testament to how human this man before him was. "I- I've missed you, as well."

A startled chuckle escaped his father's lips and he promptly dissolved into a paroxysm of coughing.

Lucien lunged out of his seat and looked about. A pitcher of water rested on a nightstand beside his bed. He picked it up and poured a glass full.

"Bah, water won't cure me, boy," his father said with a trace of dry humor he'd shown throughout the course of his life.

Nonetheless, he sat at the edge of his father's bed and braced him against his body helping him into a sitting position. Water sloshed over the rim of the glass, dampening the crisp, white bedsheets. He damned the loss of his arm that made his movements unsteady. Only, he knew as one who'd been forced to confront the many lies he'd told these five, nearly six years now, the tremble in his body had nothing to do with the absent limb. "Here," he murmured, holding the glass to his father's lips.

The viscount sipped, the muscles of his throat moving slowly, displaying an agonizing effort to manage something as simple as a swallow. A sheen of tears blurred Lucien's vision and he blinked them back. He set the glass down and eased his father back down upon the pillow. "I am so sorry."

It took a moment to register that soft plea for forgiveness belonged to his proud sire and not his own.

"I—"

"Don't," Lucien said ravaged by the sight of his parent's suffering.

His father stretched out once strong, now frail, fingers. Green veins stood out stark in his pale white skin. He touched that skeleton-like hand to Lucien's empty sleeve. "My boy," he said on a broken sob and then his gaunt frame shook under the force of his weeping.

Lucien folded him in his embrace. This man who'd put him astride his first mount and sacked the first and last tutor to ever lay a hand upon him. "Don't, please don't," he said, his words a hoarse entreaty. How many years had he lay blame at his father's feet? Upon his return, he'd taken an unholy delight in holding him responsible for everything Lucien had lost. "It was not your fault." Only now, Lucien could not, with his sire at the end of his life, leave him with the weight of that guilt.

"I-it was. A-all of it." He dissolved into a fit of coughing and Lucien held him close, fearing the older man would break under the weight of his arm. "I at least owed you a letter informing you of Sara's and M-Matthew's deaths. I'd thought…" A spasm of agony ravaged his father's face. "I thought to protect you from that truth."

Lucien waited for the bitterness at that great irony: the man who'd sent his son off to fight a bloody war had sought to protect him from the contents of a missive about his family. Only, the flood of resentment did not come. "It is done," he said softly, the words spoken more to himself.

"W-what a waste." His father's words, the faintest whisper, reached Lucien's ears.

"Indeed it was." He stared over the top of his father's head at the soft blue, plaster walls. How very close he'd been to never again seeing one of the parents who'd given him life. And he wouldn't have. If it hadn't been for Eloise. "I almost didn't come," he said quietly.

His father sucked in several long, shallow breaths and Lucien thought he slept. "Richard believed Eloise would find you. He said the Devil himself couldn't bring you here." A softness lit his eyes and dimmed the agony of dying reflected within their depths. "But that Eloise could."

Lucien glanced across the room at the closed door, feeling her presence even through the thick, wood panel, reassured in just knowing she was there.

"That girl has loved you as long as she's known you," his father said with all the sage wisdom of a man who saw and knew all. "Come, nothing to say?" For a moment, he spoke with the same bold strength that Lucien long remembered and he allowed himself the all too brief moment of believing that they two were the same men they'd been before a madman had ravaged the Continent and ultimately destroyed their family.

His father waggled a brow.

Lucien cleared his throat. "I know."

His father coughed into his hand. Lucien leapt to his feet to get the half-filled glass but his father waved him off. "I always imagined you'd wed Ellie," his father said softly, more to himself. A pained smile wreathed his gaunt cheeks. "Then, perhaps that was just my own wishful musings for the both of you."

Lucien stared down at his lone hand, the callused pads of his fingers, the scars marring his flesh from the spray of shrapnel at the Battle of Fuentes de Onoro.

"She's always been loyal to you," his father continued.

He may as well have had a dog then...

Yes, she had been steadfast in her devotion since the moment he'd instructed her on how to plant someone a facer, but his love for her went beyond those mere sentiments of loyalty. He loved her for her resilience, her courage, her—

"I don't know another lady who would have stayed to care for an ailing woman and child the way she did for Sara and Matthew." The raspy words cut into his thoughts.

He blinked and picked his head up. "What?"

The viscount closed his eyes. His chest contracted with each struggled breath he drew. "You didn't know that?" he asked. His lids fluttered open. A ghost of a smile hovered on his gaunt cheeks. "Of course, you didn't. Ellie would never be one to extol her own deeds." A spasm of pain wracked his face. "The doctor, useless man," he mumbled, "claimed nothing could be done to save them."

The pain of that loss would always, always be with him and yet, at his father's words, the familiar jagged agony that could cut a man to the core—did not come. At some point, Eloise had breathed life into a body he'd thought long dead. Then, the slow-turning wheels of his mind processed his father's words. "She was here?" Eloise would have been recently married.

"Eloise and her husband were visiting," his father said, confirming his supposition. He flexed his wrist in a feeble attempt to wave his hand about. "She did that, you know. Most ladies would forget about their father's friends. Godfather or not." The viscount closed his eyes again.

He should halt the flow of his father's words, preserve his energy but, bastard that he was, Lucien needed to hear the remainder of this story he didn't know and likely never would have…if he hadn't come home.

"Eloise went to your home." Odd to think of that modest dwelling upon the viscount's property as home. He and Sara had lived there but a handful of months before he marched off to face Boney's men. "She remained there when the doctor said it was futile. Cared for them until the end."

His father's words sucked the air from his lungs. "She never said anything," he whispered. Why? He shot a glance over to the door separating them. Why would she keep that from him? He fumbled about for an explanation but came up empty.

"Fell quite ill herself," his father murmured. "The doctor thought she would not make it." He smiled and the muscles ticking in the corner of his lips indicated the effort that happy gesture cost him. "Eloise has more strength than most grown men I know." He grimaced at the exertion of speaking those handful of meaningful words.

Lucien sank back in his seat in silent shock. In spite of her elevated status as countess, Eloise had gone to his wife's side. She had nursed Sara and his son and nearly paid with the price of her life for that great sacrifice. Agony twisted in his belly. He cupped his hand over his mouth. In all his miserable years, there had been but one thing he was right about—he didn't deserve her.

"Lucien?" His father sucked air noisily through his lips.

He rested his hand on his father's. "Rest," he entreated, willing him to a peaceful silence.

137

Then with a shocking display of strength, he chuckled. "I've the whole of eternity to rest." His father gave him a stern look that melted away the years of difference between them and Lucien was son, and the viscount was father. "Send in Eloise."

TWENTY

Eloise stared at the closed panel door with a blend of grief and panicked trepidation. All the old memories rushed to the surface and she closed her eyes to ebb their rapid flow. Her efforts proved ineffectual. The stench of bodies fevered in their sweat permeated her senses, the biting scent pungent even after all these years. Her mouth went dry. She could not enter the viscount's chambers. Even as he'd been like another father to her through the years, she could not step through that door and bear the sight of more death, more suffering…

Richard took her hand and gave it a firm, reassuring squeeze that drew her from the edge of the nightmares. "Eloise, how can I ever repay you?"

She returned her focus to the door and instead of the scent of death and sickness, she focused on the reunion between father and son that now occurred on the other side of the panel. Surely theirs was not a contentious meeting. It couldn't be at this final moment. "I haven't done anything." Richard and Palmer hadn't seen Lucien in years. They'd been spared proof of the hardened man he'd become.

Richard captured her hands in his, giving a faint squeeze. "Surely you know none of this would have happened if it hadn't been for you." A spasm of pain contorted his face. "My father would have died and both he and Lucien would have lost that much needed peace they both deserve." A peace they all deserved. "How did you convince him to come?"

She sighed. "In a way I'm not at all proud of."

He opened his mouth to say something on it, but the door opened. They swung their gazes to the door. Lucien stood framed in the entrance, his narrow-eyed stare on Eloise's hands clasped in Richard's. She released them suddenly.

"He's asked for Eloise," Lucien said, his tone gave little indication to his thoughts.

Her mouth went dry with fear and she inched away. "I…" Can't. She could not step foot into another room of death. Eloise pressed her eyes closed and then opened them. She might not want to enter that room but she *could* do this. For the man who'd been like another father to her. For her father who'd had no better friend in all his life. And for Lucien and, of course, his brothers. She could do this for them.

With head held high, she started for the door. Lucien remained rooted to his spot, blocking her entrance. He took in her face and then looked over her person as though verifying that she was, in fact, all right. Which was quite preposterous. He didn't know of the terror she still carried in her heart or the irrational guilt for her inability to help his wife and son.

Wordlessly, he stepped aside.

Eloise curled her hands so tight, her nails left indents upon the soft skin of her palms, biting into the flesh hard enough to draw blood. The need for his support in this perhaps last and final visit with the viscount was a physical hungering. She took a step forward and he shot his hand out, taking her fingers in his. She glanced down at their interlocked fingers and then raised her gaze to his. Something charged and volatile passed between them. And then, he released her.

She entered the room, the lingering scent of death hung on the air. She pressed her eyes closed as the deaths of her father, Sara, and Matthew crept around her mind.

"Eloise?"

Eloise hovered at the doorway and tried to set aside memories of past loss. "Yes, Lord Hereford." She closed the door partway and cautiously made her way over to the bed.

The viscount, once bold and proud, struggled to push himself up onto his elbows. Reservations aside, she raced over. "Please, don't," she said. "Rest."

He coughed noisily and gestured to the vacant seat. She sat. Perched on the edge of her chair she took his frail hand in hers. The ghost of a smile played about his lips. "Do you know," he began so faintly she struggled to hear. "I always wanted a daughter."

"You and Papa were always a wonderful match." She gave his hands a gentle squeeze. "He always wanted a son."

"Ah, but there you are wrong." He shook his head. "He always needed a son…but he always wanted a daughter." A gleam twinkled in his pained eyes. "As did I." His gaze skittered off to the door. "Don't tell my sons," he said with traces of the humor he'd shown through the years that made her forget a moment that she sat here now paying her last respects to this loyal friend of her late father's.

Eloise leaned over and whispered close to his ear, "Your secret is safe with me."

They shared another smile.

"Oh, Eloise, I am so very grateful to you." The hollow lines of his throat moved with his audible swallow. "You brought my son back to me."

"I didn't do that," she said softly. "He was ready to come home." He'd just required a gentle reminder.

"Do you know, the greatest regret of my life was buying that commission for him?"

Eloise said nothing, all the while wishing she could draw forth the comforting words he deserved at the end of his life. She set the viscount's hand down upon the crisp, white linen. Yet, she shared that very same regret. She wished Lucien had never left his wife and son. Then mayhap he'd not have been consumed by so many bitter resentments.

"Do you know my second great regret?"

"What is that?" she murmured.

"That not one of my boys was wise enough to wed you." He dissolved into another fit of coughing.

Eloise hopped to her feet and picked up the nearby pitcher from the side table. She filled his glass then set the porcelain jug down. "Here," she said. She reclaimed her seat and held the glass up to his lips.

He took slow, laborious sips. "Think to distract me do you?" He waggled an eyebrow.

Her lips twitched. "Did it work?"

"Not at all." He held up a bent finger and waved it about "We were talking about my foolish sons."

"They're not foolish," she said loyally. As much as she'd longed for Lucien, time had forced her to confront the truth—he loved another. And she'd loved him enough to let go of the dream of him as anything more...but that friend from long ago.

"I always imagined you would marry Lucien." He spoke more to himself. "In my life, I never saw such a bond between a man and woman the way you two shared. Even as children..." He coughed once again. "Even as children," he repeated. "You had a friendship unlike I've ever known."

"Most boys would detest a young girl who made a nuisance of herself, the way I did." And at first, Lucien the boy had chafed at her bothersome presence.

The viscount's words cut into her musings. "He loves you."

She didn't doubt Lucien did, and always had, loved her as a friend. "I know," she assured him. She'd merely ached for more.

He shook his head. "He *loves* you," he said, a meaningful look in his blue eyes.

Eloise warmed at the significance of his supposition. "Oh, no," she said hurriedly. She looked to the door and then back to the viscount. "Never as he loved Sara. Perhaps as a dear sister." Except the memory of his kiss still burned like an indelible imprint upon her lips. His was the kiss a man gave to a lover.

He rested his hand upon hers and she started. "He does," he said, his voice weakening.

Suddenly discomfited by the personal direction of Lord Hereford's words, she stood. "You must rest, my lord."

He managed a nod. "Mark my words, Eloise. He'll find the courage to profess his love and I'll be smiling all the way to the hereafter."

The viscount stilled and for one horrific, endless span of a heart-beat she believed he'd died. But then the faint, almost imperceptible inhalation as he drew breath indicated he still lived. Eloise padded quietly across the room. She slipped outside into the hall.

Richard and Lucien stood, in like positions—feet braced apart, somber sets to the harsh, angular planes of their faces. But for Lucien's missing limb, with their dark hair and storm gray eyes, they may as well have been mirror images of one another.

They looked expectantly at her. "He is sleeping."

Some of the tension left Richard's shoulders. Lucien, however, remained so still he gave no indication as to his thoughts.

"You should rest, Eloise," Richard comforted breaking the silence.

Her skin prickled with awareness of Lucien's gaze upon her person. Yet, he said nothing, continuing to stare at her with that probing, intense look she'd come to expect. Eloise nodded, wanting Lucien to say something, needing him to.

Yet, as Richard led her down the hall to her guest chambers, Lucien maintained his cool silence.

TWENTY-ONE

T he next morning, Palmer ordered the bell tolled six times to signify the viscount was near passing. By the afternoon, he sucked in a final, labored, gasping breath and then slipped into the next world. Shortly thereafter, the funeral furnisher employed by Palmer in anticipation of the viscount's passing, arrived to set the formal burial plans into motion.

With the day gone, ushered in by the black of night, Lucien sat numbly in the quiet of the Blue Parlor now somberly draped with black baize. The candles placed about the room cast eerie shadows. For the lives he'd taken down in the field of battle and the loss he'd known of his wife and child, he'd imagined himself immune to any further pain. Staring at his father's unmoving, lifeless form—he realized one never truly became accustomed to the eternal permanence of death.

Since he'd set himself up as vigil, shutting himself in with his father until tomorrow when the viscount would be formally buried in the family burial grounds, his own life had played out before him in the silence of the room.

He could place his life neatly into two categories. The unfettered happiness he'd known as a young man, unmarred physically, mentally, and emotionally by war...and everything to come after the commission that had been purchased. Lucien shoved himself to his feet and wandered closer to his father's now peaceful form. He would forever bear the scars of the life he'd lived. The war had changed him, as had the loss of his wife and son.

But who was he now? The Marchioness of Drake had drawn him back from the precipice of despair in which death had been preferable to life. She and her husband had given him work and through that, purpose. A reason to wake up, put one leg in front of the other, and exist.

He'd not realized that he wanted more than to merely exist—until Eloise. Lucien took the final steps between him and his father. He brushed his knuckles along the expertly tailored, black coat prepared by the man's loyal valet. Just eight days ago, he would have both celebrated in his death and envied him that final rest. Now, since Eloise, he was forced to confront all the empty pieces of his own life. The viscount had left two sons, prosperous landholdings, and through Palmer and his wife, future offspring.

How very empty, how very alone Lucien's life was.

It doesn't have to be, an enticing voice whispered.

There was a woman, a woman he didn't deserve, who'd been loyal and loving. He swiped his hand over his face. She'd been a girl just out in London and for her station and young years, cared for his wife and child, sat beside them, until they'd drawn their last breaths.

You never held someone in your arms while they died. You never knew the agony as that person sucked in a final breath and was no more...

Those cruel, erroneous words he'd hurled at her mocked him. For that, she'd still maintained her silence. How many other things had he been wrong about where Eloise was concerned? She'd opened his eyes and, in her, he saw a world of things he'd not imagined for himself—happiness, love, a child—all became tangible dreams within his grasp.

Nay, not just any child. A precious, stubborn girl with tight, blonde curls. "You would have liked that, wouldn't you?" he asked quietly.

Of course, there was no answer. No reaction. Nothing but the absolutism of death's dark quiet. He drew his hand back.

The floorboards creaked and he stiffened.

"Lucien," Eloise said softly, her greeting, one word, his name drifted over.

The rustle of satin skirts filled the room. He cast a glance down at the slender slip of a woman who sidled up to him with a crimson

145

bouquet of poppies wilted in her hands. She'd donned black mourning attire. Again. His heart wrenched in at last setting aside all the grief he'd known these years to confront the tragedy in a woman of her young age wearing these same dark skirts to bury her husband and then father.

"Eloise," he murmured. "What—?"

"I came to pay my respects." As always, she interpreted his unfinished thoughts with an uncanniness that spanned the course of their relationship. "To say goodbye," she added as an afterthought. She set the poppies they'd picked yesterday, yesteryear, a lifetime ago, upon the viscount's chest.

He blamed the exhaustion of their travels and lack of sleep for the swell of emotion that clogged his throat. "I cannot ever repay what you've done." She'd allowed him a small measure, but an important measure, of peace.

Eloise touched her fingers to his cheek. "There is nothing to repay, Lucien. You are my friend," she said simply.

His gut clenched. She'd claimed to love him, to want more of him. Perhaps she'd wisely realized there were any number of more suitable options; all of whom had never lain prone in a hospital bed, wallowing for years in the misery of their lives, and then taken on the work as a servant.

"He was a good man," Eloise said. A sorrowful smile tugged her lips ever so slightly upwards. Her sadness with those words caused a vise-like pressure to tighten about his lungs and make it difficult to draw a steady breath. "When we were children and played hide and go seek, he would allow me to hide in his office." She gave him a look and her smile widened. "Most men would have sacked the nursemaid for allowing a child to be underfoot." She lovingly stroked the viscount's cold, lifeless hand folded in front of him. "But then I was always so curious." She had been. About everything. "I would tire of you searching for me and sit in his enormous office chair and ask him a thousand and one questions. All of which he answered." A golden tress fell across her eye. She brushed it back. "Odd how often I spent waiting for you to find me." A shift occurred in their conversation. Her words transcended mere children's games.

Tell her. His father's booming voice bounced around the walls of his mind as clear as if he now spoke before them, so much so that he froze and glanced about.

"What is it?" she asked, following his gaze.

Regardless, this was not the place or time and the words withered on the faint echo of a memory of his father's voice. "It is nothing." The fire cracked and hissed in the hearth. "My father told me what you did, Eloise."

Her narrow shoulders went taut. "What I—?"

He brushed his knuckles along her jaw. Even now she'd not share in the truth of her great sacrifice. "Come, Ellie, you know." For years he'd thought only of himself and his hurts and regrets, and all along Eloise had been there, loving, caring for his wife, his son, his entire family. He was humbled by her selflessness and shamed by his total unworthiness of her. "I refer to what you did for Sara." He braced for all the old hurts at the mention of his wife's name. Hurt that did not come.

Eloise wetted her lips. "You know?" Soft surprise underscored her question.

He nodded once. "I know."

Eloise angled her chin up, as though braced for his criticism. "You would have done the same for me."

Ah, God, he was undeserving of her faith and devotion. Regret twisted inside him. He clenched and unclenched his jaw. For would he truly have done the same? From the moment the new vicar had entered the village with his winsome daughter, Lucien had not been the friend Eloise deserved—the friend he'd once been. Hell, he'd not even known her husband's name, how they'd met, any details of the courtship preceding her marriage. Her husband, who'd seen her cared for in his passing had been a better, far more worthy man for Eloise than Lucien ever could have been. Perhaps fate had known that. Shame stuck in his throat and made it impossible to speak.

147

She cleared her throat. "It is late." When had Ellie Gage ever worried about things such as time? She held his gaze and then with infinite slowness moved her eyes over his face as though committing him to memory. "As I said, I came to say my goodbyes."

Lucien caught her hand in his and raised it to his lips. "Not goodbye, Eloise. Good night," he corrected.

A sheen covered her eyes and she blinked rapidly. Then as quick as they'd come, the crystalline drops were gone.

Without another word, Eloise pulled her hand free and left.

He stared after her. She didn't realize that, if she would allow him, there would never be another parting between them.

TWENTY-TWO

Three weeks later

With the Marquess of Drake's horse returned weeks prior, Lucien, in his brother's carriage now, made the lonely return to London, along the rain splattered streets of the city. After nearly a day's worth of rain, the thick, gray storm clouds had parted. He tugged the curtain back distractedly and peered out at the familiar passing scenes and he reflected on Eloise.

Odd, he'd gone years not noticing Eloise and now, he saw her everywhere. Including something as simple as a carriage ride. The memory as she'd been seated across from him, sopping wet from the cold rain, her cheeks wan from the motion of the carriage roused pained regret inside him.

The night Eloise had come to pay her respects and make her goodbyes to his father, the Viscount Hereford, Lucien had failed to realize that he was, in fact, the person she'd bid fare thee well to. And for all the years of having failed to notice Eloise Gage, this keen, awareness of the woman she'd become, had made the loss of her all the greater.

With her parting, he'd been forced to navigate the former relationships he'd once known as brother to men he considered his closest friends and ultimately became strangers by decisions he himself had made. Eloise had opened his eyes to so very much including the realization that for all that had come between him and his family, they were still his family. The years had melted away and despite the grief of their loss, there too had been the assurance in at last knowing one another as friends and brothers. Again, it was because of Eloise. All because of her.

The carriage rocked to a slow halt and he stared out the window at the familiar London townhouse—the place he'd resided, worked, and called home for two years. He'd left this very townhouse angry and furious. Furious at Eloise for her interference. Furious at life for having taken so much from him. Furious with being forced from the one place he'd managed to find a shred of peace after the war.

Now he returned, a changed man. A man who'd been forced to confront the demons in his life and if not destroy, then conquer them enough to live a life devoid of the agonized pain that would have slowly destroyed him.

The driver pulled open the door. Lucien made to step down. He held the edge of the doorway and paused a moment. The reservations crept in, their tentacle-like fingers crept around his brain, reminding him the inferiority of a limbless man amidst a world of glittering perfection.

A flash of sunshine streamed through the thick clouds overhead and spilled light upon the metal lions of the Marquess of Drake's door-knocker. It was time. Time to resume living—fully. Lucien climbed down and strode with purposeful steps up the stairs. He knocked. He turned and stared out momentarily at the quiet London streets, waiting for the man who now held his post and likely would continue to hold his post after he left.

The door opened. The young under butler, Gatwick, opened his mouth to greet him and then blinked. "Mr. Jones," he said slowly. He ran his gaze over Lucien's immaculate, fawn colored breeches and sapphire blue coat, the stark, white cravat. He opened and closed his mouth several times. "Mr. Jones," he repeated again and then scrambled over himself in his haste to allow Lucien entry.

He grinned. "I'm here to speak to the marquess."

Gatwick closed the door. "Of course, of course." He took a step forward and then faltered. "Er…" He scratched his brow as he tried to navigate Lucien's now uncertain role—butler or visitor.

He relieved the other man of his difficulty. "The marquess is…?"

"In his office, Mr. Jones."

Lucien inclined his head. "I shall see to it. As you were, Gatwick."

The younger servant bowed and backed away.

Lucien stared after him a moment. The men and women here had never been a family to him. He'd not allowed himself a connection with anyone after he'd lost Sara and Matthew. Instead, he'd constructed walls about his heart to protect himself, until Eloise had taken them apart in her capable hands one bitter memory at a time. And yet, in this next parting, there was a new loss, a passing of a life he'd lived, that second phase of his life, the dark, lonely world he'd embraced all these years.

But it was time. Lucien started through the foyer, footsteps silent upon the white marble floor. It was time to move forward and begin again. He curled his hand at his side. If she would let him. If it wasn't too late. How many opportunities had he had with Eloise and how many times had he ignored and rejected the beautiful offering of her?

He turned right down the corridor and strode along the long, empty hall. What if she rejected him? Which by all intents and purposes, she should do. What was he without her? Lucien paused outside the marquess' office. He'd been a coward long enough. It was time to go to her and offer her all he was capable, all he was, all he had, which in the scheme of what she was worth and entitled to—was nothing.

He knocked once.

"Enter," the marquess called out.

Lucien stepped inside.

Lord Drake glanced up from his ledgers and stilled. "Jonas," he said, surprise laced the statement.

And staring at the usually unflappable young lord, it occurred to him—the marquess hadn't believed he would return. He'd known. "Captain," he said bowing. Just as the marquess had known how to restore him to the living, so too had he known his time here was at an end.

The marquess surged to his feet. "Come in. Come in." He gestured to the seat across from his desk.

Lucien strolled over, for the first time conscious of his change in status. Even with the remembered proper tones and properly tailored garments, he still was that coarse, battle weary soldier who'd first met the other man upon the fields of Europe...and then again within the bleak walls of London Hospital. He sat.

Lord Drake reclaimed his seat. Lucien drummed his fingertips along the side of his boots. The marquess' gaze took in the armband on Lucien's left sleeve. "I'm sorry for the loss of your father," he said quietly. "My condolences."

Lucien stilled his distracted movement. "Thank you." He paused. "And thank you for," *forcing* "encouraging me to go." Lord Drake was just another he'd be forever indebted to. It had taken a number of people to put together the empty, shattered pieces of Lucien Jonas— Lady Drake, Lord Drake, the nurses at London Hospital. But he would never have been whole again. Not without Eloise. She was the missing piece in his life and at last he was complete. He drew in a breath. If she'd have him..."I considered your offer, my lord. The role of steward."

The marquess arched an eyebrow. "And?"

He held his palm up. "And I believe my role is elsewhere." It was with Eloise. It always had been. It had only taken him a lifetime to realize it. "With my father's passing, he deeded me property." And in doing so, had given him a renewed purpose, a sense of independence, and more, placed him in a position where he deserved a lady...or more specifically—a countess. Though there was everything honorable in the work he'd taken on in the marquess' employ, that role would preclude him from having that which he truly wanted. "I am not so naïve that I imagine it shall be an easy charge, taking over the running of an estate." He gave a lopsided grin and gestured to the empty place his arm had been. "Then, I imagine with everything I've lost and faced in life, this should be the easier role I've taken on."

They shared a look; two men who'd seen done, and still dreamed and saw horrible things. "I do not disagree with you." Lord Drake sat back in his seat. "Would you be startled were I to tell you that I agree with you?" He folded his arms across his chest. "You belong elsewhere and more importantly, with a particular someone."

He allowed his silence to mark his confirmation.

The marquess shoved back his seat. He angled his head toward the door. "Now, I imagine you've more important things to attend than speaking with me." He held a hand out.

Lucien studied it a moment and then stood. He shook the marquess' hand. "Thank you," he said quietly. For giving him purpose. For thrusting him back into a world he'd sworn to never again be a part of.

The other man gave a slight, imperceptible nod, the meaningful look in his eyes indicating he'd followed Lucien's unspoken thoughts.

With that, he turned on his heel and started from the room, walking from his past and into—

Lady Drake stepped around the corner. He collided with the young marchioness. Lucien bit back a curse. "Forgive me, my lady," he said quickly.

She waved off his concern, giving him a gentle smile. "Lieutenant Jones." She took in his fine apparel, the expert lines of his cravat, his gleaming black boots, and then met his eyes. "Why do I imagine your time here is at an end?"

Because it was. He looked to her, this woman who'd distracted him enough to save his life. "Thank you," he said simply, the words wholly inadequate to convey the gratitude for all she'd done. "If you'd not persisted," Her lips quirked at the corners in remembrance of those words he'd once hurled at her angrily from within the confines of his bed at London Hospital. "I'd not be alive now."

She shook her head. "Oh, I don't believe that." Lady Drake continued over him when he opened his mouth to protest. "You wouldn't have..." *Killed yourself.* She let those sinful words go unspoken. "You had a reason to live, even if you didn't realize it at the time."

He started as she took his hand between her gloved fingers, recalling his attention. "You realize it now and that is what matters."

"It is likely too late," he said, gut clenching. What if it was? What was he without her?

She gave his hand a squeeze. "I know better than anyone else that time really means nothing in the matters of the heart. You know now." A sparkle glimmered in her kind, brown eyes. "I know your Eloise. She knows. Go to her."

"Thank you," he said, firm resolve underscored his words. "I intend to." Even if she rejected him and called him a fool for having failed to notice her, truly notice her, he needed to tell her. And if she'd allow him, he'd spend the rest of his life loving her, as she'd always deserved.

Lady Emmaline gave a pleased nod and then released him. "Go," she urged.

He looked at her a lingering moment—this woman, her husband, this townhouse a link to his recent, dark, and lonely past. Lucien turned and nodded at Lord Drake as they shared a look that only two men who'd faced down the Devil and survived, might understand. He shifted his attention to Lady Emmaline; the person who'd not allowed him to turn himself over to darkness. How could he ever repay either her or her husband? They'd restored him to the living, and in that, guided him back to Eloise. "I—" He opened and closed his mouth several times. "I—"

A gentle smile turned Lady Drake's lips upwards. "I know." She tipped her chin toward the door. "Go to her."

With a final bow, he shook free the chains of his past and left—ready to embrace his future.

TWENTY-THREE

A thunderous shout penetrated the walls of Eloise's parlor. With an aggrieved sigh, she set aside the book in her hands. It had been inevitable. Since she'd returned from the viscount's, she'd felt with a confidence she'd have wagered everything she had right to as a widow, that word of her scandalous carriage ride with Lucien and their foray through the field of flowers would inevitably make its way to her brother-in-law. She'd just imagined it would have been weeks ago.

The sharp click of boot steps in the hall, increasing in fervor, paused outside of the parlor.

She shoved herself to her feet just as the butler, opened the door. "The Earl of Sherborne," he intoned, his face an expressionless mask.

Eloise donned her winningest smile. "Why, Lord Sherborne, what a—"

"This is not about pleasantries, Eloise," he snapped. It never was with the new earl.

The butler took his leave, but not before favoring her with a regretful look.

Eloise gestured to the sofa. "Would you care to sit?"

Lips set in a tense, angry line, her brother-in-law stalked over. "I do not care to sit, madam. I care about my reputation, as it is affected by your scandalous actions."

For his ill opinion, she'd venture there wasn't a more scandal-less widow than she.

"I assure you, I'm everything proper," she said dryly.

The earl either ignored or failed to hear the wry edge to her words. "I've heard whispers amongst my household staff of your carrying on with a Mr. Lucien Jonas." He planted his hands upon his hips and towered over her. "My brother—"

"Your brother would take offense at your storming into my home and scolding me like a recalcitrant child," she shot back. His high-handedness these years had grown tedious.

At her bold rebuttal, shock stamped the lines of his face. He opened and closed his mouth. "Why, I…I…"

Emboldened by his shock, Eloise took a step forward. "Why do you, indeed, my lord? Why do you believe it is your right to enter my townhouse and chide me for behaviors reported about by gossiping servants?"

"Because it matters to my own reputation," he thundered. His booming voice bounced off the high ceilings. "I am in the market for a countess." The poor woman. She felt the stirring of pity for that unknown lady. "And," he waved his finger in a circle in her general direction. "And as long as mention of you tupping servants is fodder for the gossips, the more you sully the Sherborne title."

Eloise's cheeks flamed with a scorching heat at his crude words. His reprehensible charge quelled her tart response.

"Ah, nothing to say?" He made a tsking sound. "Rumors have circulated about your carrying on with the Marquess of Drake's one-armed butler."

She gasped. A red rage descended over her vision, blinding in its intensity. "Remember yourself," she bit out. She'd often said that all the goodness in the Sherborne line had been given to that first-born son, Colin, her husband, leaving none left for this cruel, cowardly, current Earl of Sherborne.

"Remember myself?" His eyes flew wide. "You, my lady, are the one sullying your reputation by spreading your legs for a mere servant."

Eloise cracked her hand across his cheek with such ferocity, her palm imprinted upon his skin.

"By God! My brother will be turning over in the hereafter with—"

"If I were you, I would allow those words to go unfinished."

Eloise wheeled around. Her pulse thundered madly as Lucien's well-muscled frame filled the entranceway. Her brother-in-law stiffened at the unexpected intrusion.

The butler cleared his throat. "Mr. Lucien Jonas," he announced. The ghost of a smile played about the normally unflappable butler's lips. He dipped a bow and then backed out of the room.

"Wh-what is the meaning of this?" the earl stammered. He retreated as Lucien advanced with slow, deliberate strides into the parlor.

The sight of him after all these weeks blotted out the humiliating, horrible things leveled at her by the earl. "L-Lucien," she whispered. *Why is he here?* Why, when he'd been so very clear that after his father's passing he would return to the life he'd lived all these years without her?

Her brother-in-law found his brash arrogance. "Why are you here, sir?" He puffed his chest like a preening peacock. "There is no room for a mere butler—"

"You'd be wise to not finish those words, either," Lucien intoned on a silken, steely whisper.

The color drained from the earl's cheeks. He found the courage, however to tug at his jacket and say, "I am the Earl of Sherborne and I'll not be spoken to in…"

Lucien continued striding forward and the lean bully of a man stumbled over himself in his haste to place the sofa between him and the threatening gentleman. Lucien stopped beside Eloise. He passed that inscrutable, powerful stare over her face, the grays of his eyes dark like the summer sky after a tempestuous storm.

Then, with seeming reluctance, he shifted his focus back upon the earl. "You are to leave this home, Sherborne. And you are no longer to sully Eloise with your presence here. If you speak to her," he said, as he stepped around the mahogany piece between them and then closed the distance between him and her bastard of a brother-in-law. "If you so much as speak to her, I will demonstrate just how capable I am with one arm," He lowered his tone to the gravelly, harsh one that had initially terrified her upon their reunion at the marquess' home. "And I will make you regret whatever vile word you uttered." He leaned close. "Are we clear, Sherborne?"

The earl's cheeks turned ashen and in spite of the obvious quake to his slender frame, he managed a jerky nod.

Eloise's heart tripped several beats at his bold defense of her. She pressed her eyes closed a moment. She'd been on her own for so very long, she'd grown accustomed to relying on no one but herself. She opened her eyes once more and caressed Lucien with her gaze. For the first time in a long time, she was not alone. Joy swelled inside and a wave of emotion so strong slammed into her that she could not speak. Her throat worked painfully.

Lucien looked at Sherborne through eyes of impenetrable slits and then gave a belated nod. "You're done here." He stepped aside and her brother-in-law all but sprinted from the room. With his awkward gait, the earl knocked into a side table and then upended an ivory, open-backed armchair before scurrying from the room like a rat chased from Cook's kitchens.

Her shoulders sagged with relief at the man's exit. However, with his parting and the vitriol of Lucien's exchange, she registered his presence. She fiddled with her skirts. "Lucien."

"Is that all you'll say?" His deep baritone washed over her.

Eloise stilled her distracted movements. "Hullo?"

He closed the slight space between them. "I suppose that is a good deal better than *get out*," he said dryly. He raised his hand, his knuckles hovered awkwardly at her cheek, and then he dropped his hand back to his side.

Eloise mourned the loss of that slight, desperately desired touch. "Wh-why would I order you to leave?" She loved him and always would. She would take him in any way she could—even if he was merely a visiting friend.

A humorless grin hovered at his lips. "Perhaps because you should order me gone."

She shook her head. "I'd not do that."

"Not even if I deserve it?"

"Why would you deserve it? Because you never loved me the way I loved you?" She bit the inside of her cheek, the startling honesty of that admission twisted her insides. Suddenly, his body's nearness was too much. She wandered over to the ivory sofa and trailed her finger-tips over the mahogany back.

"I—"

She held a hand up. "You loved and married. I'd never begrudge you the happiness you knew." Even as the lost dream of him had shredded her heart.

"I—"

"I long ago accepted that anything more between us, it was a mere dream, Lucien." The truth of her words twisted like a blade in her belly. She hugged her arms to herself. "I knew that, even as my heart did not." Except, even now she lied to herself. Her love of Lucien defied all logic and knowing. It was based on friendship and emotion and those undefinable sentiments only carried deep within a person's heart.

"Eloise, I—"

She curled her hands over the back of the sofa and studied her white-knuckled grip upon the furniture. "You don't need to apologize," she assured him, picking up her gaze, she met his stare directly.

"I'm not here to apologize." Heavy regret shaded his words.

Oh. Warmth crept up her neck and heated her cheeks. "Uh. Well, then." She shifted awkwardly on her feet. "Why are you here?" she blurted and then at the frown on his lips she added, "Not that I'm not incredibly happy to see you." Regardless of his feelings or lack of feelings for her, she would, always be filled with joy at seeing him. Even when he was snarly and angry and foul. "I am," she added as afterthought.

His eyebrows dipped.

"Happy to see you," she clarified. "I'm merely..." *Rambling. You're rambling, Eloise.*

Lucien strolled over, impossibly cool and hopelessly elegant with his long, graceful movements. He stopped in front of her with the sofa between them. "May I speak?"

She nodded.

"I didn't come to apologize," he added.

Eloise sighed. "I know. You said as—"

"Eloise."

"Er, right, sorry," she said on a rush. "You were saying?"

Lucien reached his hand across the space dividing them and cupped her cheek. "I'm not here to apologize because every apology I make will be inadequate and you deserve so much more than that." She leaned into his caress. The expensive, tailored leather glove cool and soothing upon her skin. "I was a bloody fool," he said with a directness that widened her eyes. He lowered his hand to his side. "You deserved more from me as a friend. You deserved a better man than me as your husband." He surveyed the luxurious, mahogany, Chippendale furnishings of the parlor, his gaze lingering upon the large and ornate golden bevel mirror upon the far right wall. "And I'd wager my other arm that you had him in Sherborne."

Yes, her husband had been good and more than she had deserved. But he'd never been Lucien. She'd not disrespect Colin's memory with the truth in her heart.

With a distracted movement, he picked up a porcelain shepherdess and turned it over in his hand, studying it. "My father left me property to manage—unentailed land in Kent."

Eloise tipped her head. *Is this why he's come?* She wet her lips and searched for the proper reply. "You will do splendidly in taking over the running of that estate," she said at last. For she did not doubt a moment with his intelligence and strength, he was more capable than any other landowner in the whole of England. And yet, she wished it was *more* that brought him here. Wished it *was* her.

A normally unflappable Lucien set down the shepherdess. The delicate piece wobbled on the table, then righted itself. He dragged his unsteady hand through his hair. "I've not come here to speak about the property," he paused. "Though it seems important you should know of it." He slashed the air with his hand and knocked the figurine once more. The golden-haired shepherdess tipped and fell on her side, unbroken. Lucien gave his head a shake. "That is, it seemed you should know about my acquisition of the property." Lucien frowned. "Nor have I come to apologize." His lips pulled in a grimace. "I am bumbling this."

She desperately tried to sort through his ramblings. "Bumbling wh—?"

He raised his gaze to hers, silencing her question with the burning intensity in his gray eyes. "I'm here to tell you I love you."

Her heart froze, suspended. "You…" And then the organ resumed hammering a frantic rhythm. "What?" The word emerged on a halting whisper. Lucien crossed around the sofa and stopped. "I don't understand." Because after years of loving him and dreaming for that sentiment returned, she'd long ago given up the hope of it.

The muscles of his throat worked. "You don't understand because I've been a bloody fool." He lowered his brow to hers. "It took me too long to understand that I love you, Eloise Constance. I've loved you as long as I've known you." He raised her knuckles to his mouth and brushed a kiss against them. "I just didn't realize it. I realize it now and know it's likely too late—"

"No!" The exclamation burst from her.

Eloise's denial ripped through him. No less than he warranted but still agonizing for what it represented. It had been the height of arrogance to come here and expect she should put aside the freedom she had as a widow to wed a broken, unworthy gentleman such as himself.

With pained reluctance, Lucien released her. "No," he repeated in deadened tones. He flinched at the regret tinging that one word. He'd not have her feel guilty. He gave a stiff nod and backed away. "Forgive me," his voice emerged hoarse. "I understood it was unlikely that you should indeed return my sentiments after my years of gross neglect." He took another step away from her, never removing his gaze from her person. "I will always be your devoted servant and friend." He bowed. "If you'll excuse me." With that, he hurried to the door.

"Is that all you'll say?" she called out, staying his hasty flight. "You'd just leave?"

Her words jerked him to a stop. His muscles tightened under the folds of his jacket. He turned around and looked questioningly at her.

He'd not convince her that he was worthy, because he did not himself believe it—and so he would leave.

Eloise sprinted over. She placed herself between him and the doorway. "You misunderstood me."

Lucien looked at her probingly. The first stirrings of hope fanned in a heart he'd only recently realized wasn't deadened. The organ still beat. It beat for Eloise. He spoke slowly. "I misunderstood—?"

"No it is not too late, you great lummox." The words burst from her lips. "I love you, L-Lucien," she said. Her voice broke. "I always have." She smiled tremulously up at him. "I always will."

Lucien drew in a harsh breath, and momentarily closed his eyes. "You were everything I never knew I needed, Eloise. You were always there and I never saw it."

She leaned up on tiptoes and pressed her lips to his in a slow, gentle kiss. "You see it now," she whispered. "And that is all that matters."

She was wrong. What he'd become in the years since their youth mattered. The years had changed him. War had changed him. *But then, hadn't life changed us both?* "You can love me, even as I come to you missing an arm, a man who has acted as a servant—?"

Eloise touched her fingers to his lips silencing him. "None of that matters." She moved her palm and pressed it over his heart. "This is what matters. Only this."

Ah, God. He loved her. He wanted her in his life. For now. Tomorrow. And forever. "Marry me."

She blinked, retreating a step. "What?" Her hand fluttered about her chest.

He raked his hand through his hair and cursed. "I'm making a bloody mess of this."

Eloise let her hand fall to her side. Did he imagine the ghost of a smile tugging at her lips?

He cursed. Again. "I'm cursing." He couldn't even put to her a proper offer of marriage.

Eloise's shoulders shook in clear amusement. "Uh, yes. I hear that."

He dropped to a knee. "What are you—?" Her words ended on a gasp.

"I have had three weeks to find the perfect words for you, Eloise, and, even with that, I can't manage to be what you deserved." She opened her mouth but he went on, not allowing her to speak those likely contradictory words. "Will you marry me? Marry me because I love you and I'll spend the remainder of my days showering you with every happiness you deserve." He frowned. "Though I'm not the same witty young gentleman I once was." He looked to the pinned up sleeve of his jacket. "Nor am I the young, more pleasing gentleman you likely fell in—"

A breathless laugh escaped her. "Yes, Lucien."

His heart froze and hope exploded through him. "Yes, I'm not the pleasing gentleman you fell in love with?" He stood slowly. "Or yes, you'll marry me?"

She looped her arms around his neck and leaned up. "The latter," she whispered against his mouth.

A smile turned his lips. "I love you, Eloise." He lowered his mouth to hers and claimed her lips in a gentle, searching kiss.

He was home.

The End

BIOGRAPHY

Christi Caldwell is a USA Today Bestselling author of historical romance novels set in the Regency era. Christi blames Judith McNaught's "Whitney, My Love," for luring her into the world of historical romance. While sitting in her graduate school apartment at the University of Connecticut, Christi decided to set aside her notes and try her hand at writing romance. She believes the most perfect heroes and heroines have imperfections and rather enjoys tormenting them before crafting a well-deserved happily ever after!

When Christi isn't writing the stories of flawed heroes and heroines, she can be found in her Southern Connecticut home chasing around her feisty six-year-old son, and caring for twin princesses-in-training!

Visit to learn more about what Christi is working on, or join her on Facebook at Christi Caldwell Author (for frequent updates, excerpts, and posts about her fun as a fulltime mom and writer) and Twitter (which she is still quite dreadful with).

OTHER BOOKS BY
CHRISTI CALDWELL

"Winning a Lady's Heart"
A Danby Novella

Author's Note: This is a novella that was originally available in A Summons From The Castle (The Regency Christmas Summons Collection). It is being published as an individual novella.

For Lady Alexandra, being the source of a cold, calculated wager is bad enough…but when it is waged by Nathaniel Michael Winters, 5th Earl of Pembroke, the man she's in love with, it results in a broken heart, the scandal of the season, and a summons from her grandfather – the Duke of Danby.

To escape Society's gossip, she hurries to her meeting with the duke, determined to put memories of the earl far behind. Except the duke has other plans for Alexandra…plans which include the 5th Earl of Pembroke!

"A Season of Hope"
A Danby Novella

Five years ago when her love, Marcus Wheatley, failed to return from fighting Napoleon's forces, Lady Olivia Foster buried her heart. Unable to betray Marcus's memory, Olivia has gone out of her way to run off prospective suitors. At three and twenty she considers herself firmly on the shelf. Her father, however, disagrees and accepts an offer for Olivia's hand in marriage. Yet it's Christmas, when anything can happen...

Olivia receives a well-timed summons from her grandfather, the Duke of Danby, and eagerly embraces the reprieve from her betrothal.

Only, when Olivia arrives at Danby Castle she realizes the Christmas season represents hope, second chances, and even miracles.

"Forever Betrothed, Never the Bride"
Book 1 in the Scandalous Seasons Series

Hopeless romantic Lady Emmaline Fitzhugh is tired of sitting with the wallflowers, waiting for her betrothed to come to his senses and marry her. When Emmaline reads one too many reports of his scandalous liaisons in the gossip rags, she takes matters into her own hands.

War-torn veteran Lord Drake devotes himself to forgetting his days on the Peninsula through an endless round of meaningless associations. He no longer wants to feel anything, but Lady Emmaline is making it hard to maintain a state of numbness. With her zest for life, she awakens his passion and desire for love.

The one woman Drake has spent the better part of his life avoiding is now the only woman he needs, but he is no longer a man worthy of his Emmaline. It is up to her to show him the healing power of love.

"Never Courted, Suddenly Wed"
Book 2 in the Scandalous Seasons Series

Christopher Ansley, Earl of Waxham, has constructed a perfect image for the *ton*–the ladies love him and his company is desired by all.

Only two people know the truth about Waxham's secret. Unfortunately, one of them is Miss Sophie Winters.

Sophie Winters has known Christopher since she was in leading strings. As children, they delighted in tormenting each other. Now at two and twenty, she still has a tendency to find herself in scrapes, and her marital prospects are slim.

When his father threatens to expose his shame to the *ton*, unless he weds Sophie for her dowry, Christopher concocts a plan to remain a bachelor. What he didn't plan on was falling in love with the lively, impetuous Sophie. As secrets are exposed, will Christopher's love be enough when she discovers his role in his father's scheme?

"Always Proper, Suddenly Scandalous"
Book 3 in the Scandalous Seasons Series

Geoffrey Winters, Viscount Redbrooke was not always the hard, unrelenting lord driven by propriety. After a tragic mistake, he resolved to honor his responsibility to the Redbrooke line and live a life, free of scandal. Knowing his duty is to wed a proper, respectable English miss, he selects Lady Beatrice Dennington, daughter of the Duke of Somerset, the perfect woman for him. Until he meets Miss Abigail Stone…

To distance herself from a personal scandal, Abigail Stone flees America to visit her uncle, the Duke of Somerset. Determined to never trust a man again, she is helplessly intrigued by the hard, too-proper Geoffrey. With his strict appreciation for decorum and order, he is nothing like the man' she's always dreamed of.

Abigail is everything Geoffrey does not need. She upends his carefully ordered world at every encounter. As they begin to care for one another, Abigail carefully guards the secret that resulted in her journey to England.

Only, if Geoffrey learns the truth about Abigail, he must decide which he holds most dear: his place in Society or Abigail's place in his heart.

"Always a Rogue, Forever Her Love"
Book 4 in the Scandalous Seasons Series

Miss Juliet Marshville is spitting mad. With one guardian missing, and the other singularly uninterested in her fate, she is at the mercy of her wastrel brother who loses her beloved childhood home to a man known as Sin. Determined to reclaim control of Rosecliff Cottage and her own fate, Juliet arranges a meeting with the notorious rogue and demands the return of her property.

Jonathan Tidemore, 5th Earl of Sinclair, known to the *ton* as Sin, is exceptionally lucky in life and at the gaming tables. He has just one problem. Well...four, really. His incorrigible sisters have driven off yet another governess. This time, however, his mother demands he find an appropriate replacement.

When Miss Juliet Marshville boldly demands the return of her precious cottage, he takes advantage of his sudden good fortune and puts an offer to her; turn his sisters into proper English ladies, and he'll return Rosecliff Cottage to Juliet's possession.

Jonathan comes to appreciate Juliet's spirit, courage, and clever wit, and decides to claim the fiery beauty as his mistress. Juliet, however, will be mistress for no man. Nor could she ever love a man who callously stole her home in a game of cards. As Jonathan begins to see Juliet as more than a spirited beauty to warm his bed, he realizes she could be a lady he could love the rest of his life, if only he can convince the proud Juliet that he's worthy of her hand and heart.

"A Marquess For Christmas"
Book 5 in the Scandalous Seasons Series

Lady Patrina Tidemore gave up on the ridiculous notion of true love after having her heart shattered and her trust destroyed by a black-hearted cad. Used as a pawn in a game of revenge against her brother, Patrina returns to London from a failed elopement with a tattered reputation and little hope for a respectable match. The only peace she finds is in her solitude on the cold winter days at Hyde Park. And even that is yanked from her by two little hellions who just happen to have a devastatingly handsome, but coldly aloof father, the Marquess of Beaufort. Something about the lord stirs the dreams she'd once carried for an honorable gentleman's love.

Weston Aldridge, the 4th Marquess of Beaufort was deceived and betrayed by his late wife. In her faithlessness, he's come to view women as self-serving, indulgent creatures. Except, after a series of chance encounters with Patrina, he comes to appreciate how uniquely different she is than all women he's ever known.

At the Christmastide season, a time of hope and new beginnings, Patrina and Weston, unexpectedly learn true love in one another. However, as Patrina's scandalous past threatens their future and the happiness of his children, they are both left to determine if love is enough.

"Once a Wallflower, At Last His Love"
Book 6 in the Scandalous Seasons Series

Responsible, practical Miss Hermione Rogers, has been crafting stories as the notorious Mr. Michael Michaelmas and selling them for a meager wage to support her siblings. The only real way to ensure her family's ruinous debts are paid, however, is to marry. Tall, thin, and plain, she has no expectation of success. In London for her first Season she seizes the chance to write the tale of a brooding duke. In her research, she finds Sebastian Fitzhugh, the 5th Duke of Mallen, who unfortunately is perfectly affable, charming, and so nicely...configured...he takes her breath away. He lacks all the character traits she needs for her story, but alas, any duke will have to do.

Sebastian Fitzhugh, the 5th Duke of Mallen has been deceived so many times during the high-stakes game of courtship, he's lost faith in

Society women. Yet, after a chance encounter with Hermione, he finds himself intrigued. Not a woman he'd normally consider beautiful, the young lady's practical bent, her forthright nature and her tendency to turn up in the oddest places has his interests...roused. He'd like to trust her, he'd like to do a whole lot more with her too, but should he?

"In Need of a Duke"
A Prequel Novella to "The Heart of a Duke" Series by Christi Caldwell

In Need of a Duke: (Author's Note: This is a prequel novella to "The Heart of a Duke" series by Christi Caldwell. It was originally available in "The Heart of a Duke" Collection and is now being published as an individual novella.

It features a new prologue and epilogue.

Years earlier, a gypsy woman passed to Lady Aldora Adamson and her friends a heart pendant that promised them each the heart of a duke.

Now, a young lady, with her family facing ruin and scandal, Lady Aldora doesn't have time for mythical stories about cheap baubles. She needs to save her sisters and brother by marrying a titled gentleman with wealth and power to his name. She sets her bespectacled sights upon the Marquess of St. James.

Turned out by his father after a tragic scandal, Lord Michael Knightly has grown into a powerful, but self-made man. With the whispers and stares that still follow him, he would rather be anywhere but London...

Until he meets Lady Aldora, a young woman who mistakes him for his brother, the Marquess of St. James. The connection between Aldora and Michael is immediate and as they come to know one another, Aldora's feelings for Michael war with her sisterly responsibilities. With her family's dire situation, a man of Michael's scandalous past will never do.

Ultimately, Aldora must choose between her responsibilities as a sister and her love for Michael.

"For Love of the Duke"
First Full-Length Book in the "Heart of a Duke" Series by Christi Caldwell

After the tragic death of his wife, Jasper, the 8th Duke of Bainbridge buried himself away in the dark cold walls of his home, Castle Blackwood. When he's coaxed out of his self-imposed exile to attend the amusements of the Frost Fair, his life is irrevocably changed by his fateful meeting with Lady Katherine Adamson.

With her tight brown ringlets and silly white-ruffled gowns, Lady Katherine Adamson has found her dance card empty for two Seasons. After her father's passing, Katherine learned the unreliability of men, and is determined to depend on no one, except herself. Until she meets Jasper…

In a desperate bid to avoid a match arranged by her family, Katherine makes the Duke of Bainbridge a shocking proposition—one that he accepts.

Only, as Katherine begins to love Jasper, she finds the arrangement agreed upon is not enough. And Jasper is left to decide if protecting his heart is more important than fighting for Katherine's love.

"More Than a Duke"
Book 2 in the "Heart of a Duke" Series by Christi Caldwell

Polite Society doesn't take Lady Anne Adamson seriously. However, Anne isn't just another pretty young miss. When she discovers her father betrayed her mother's love and her family descended into poverty, Anne comes up with a plan to marry a respectable, powerful, and honorable gentleman—a man nothing like her philandering father.

Armed with the heart of a duke pendant, fabled to land the wearer a duke's heart, she decides to enlist the aid of the notorious Harry, 6th Earl of Stanhope. A scoundrel with a scandalous past, he is the last gentleman she'd ever wed...however, his reputation marks him the perfect man to school her in the art of seduction so she might ensnare the illustrious Duke of Crawford.

Harry, the Earl of Stanhope is a jaded, cynical rogue who lives for his own pleasures. Having been thrown over by the only woman he ever loved so she could wed a duke, he's not at all surprised when Lady Anne approaches him with her scheme to capture another duke's affection. He's come to appreciate that all women are in fact greedy, title-grasping, self-indulgent creatures. And with Anne's history of grating on his every last nerve, she is the last woman he'd ever agree to school in the art of seduction. Only his friendship with the lady's sister compels him to help.

What begins as a pretend courtship, born of lessons on seduction, becomes something more leaving Anne to decide if she can give her heart to a reckless rogue, and Harry must decide if he's willing to again trust in a lady's love.

"The Love of a Rogue"
Book 3 in the "Heart of a Duke" Series by Christi Caldwell

Lady Imogen Moore hasn't had an easy time of it since she made her Come Out. With her betrothed, a powerful duke breaking it off to wed her sister, she's become the *tons* favorite piece of gossip. Never again wanting to experience the pain of a broken heart, she's resolved to make a match with a polite, respectable gentleman. The last thing she wants is another reckless rogue.

Lord Alex Edgerton has a problem. His brother, tired of Alex's carousing has charged him with chaperoning their remaining, unwed sister about *ton* events. Shopping? No, thank you. Attending the theatre? He'd rather be at Forbidden Pleasures with a scantily clad beauty upon his lap. The task of *chaperone* becomes even more of a bother when his sister drags along her dearest friend, Lady Imogen to social functions. The last thing he wants in his life is a young, innocent English miss.

Except, as Alex and Imogen are thrown together, passions flare and Alex comes to find he not only wants Imogen in his bed, but also in his heart. Yet now he must convince Imogen to risk all, on the heart of a rogue.

"Loved By a Duke"
Book 4 in the "Heart of a Duke" Series by Christi Caldwell

For ten years, Lady Daisy Meadows has been in love with Auric, the Duke of Crawford. Ever since his gallant rescue years earlier, Daisy knew she was destined to be his Duchess. Unfortunately, Auric sees her as his best friend's sister and nothing more. But perhaps, if she can manage to find the fabled heart of a duke pendant, she will win over the heart of her duke.

Auric, the Duke of Crawford enjoys Daisy's company. The last thing he is interested in however, is pursuing a romance with a woman he's known since she was in leading strings. This season, Daisy is turning up in the oddest places and he cannot help but notice that she is no longer a girl. But Auric wouldn't do something as foolhardy as to fall in love with Daisy. He couldn't. Not with the guilt he carries over his past sins…Not when he has no right to her heart…But perhaps, just perhaps, she can forgive the past and trust that he'd forever cherish her heart—but will she let him?

"Seduced By a Lady's Heart"
Book 1 in the "Lords of Honor" Series

You met Lieutenant Lucien Jones in "Forever Betrothed, Never the Bride" when he was a broken soldier returned from fighting Boney's forces. This is his story of triumph and happily-ever-after!

Lieutenant Lucien Jones, son of a viscount, returned from war, to find his wife and child dead. Blaming his father for the commission that sent him off to fight Boney's forces, he was content to languish at London Hospital...until offered employment on the Marquess of Drake's staff. Through his position, Lucien found purpose in life and is content to keep his past buried.

Lady Eloise Yardley has loved Lucien since they were children. Having long ago given up on the dream of him, she married another. Years later, she is a young, lonely widow who does not fit in with the ton. When Lucien's family enlists her aid to reunite father and son, she leaps at the opportunity to not only aid her former friend, but to also escape London.

Lucien doesn't know what scheme Eloise has concocted, but knowing her as he does, when she pays a visit to his employer, he knows she's up to something. The last thing he wants is the temptation that this new, older, mature Eloise presents; a tantalizing reminder of happier times and peace.

Yet Eloise is determined to win Lucien's love once and for all...if only Lucien can set aside the pain of his past and risk all on a lady's heart.

NON-FICTION WORKS BY
CHRISTI CALDWELL

Uninterrupted Joy: Memoir: My Journey through
Infertility, Pregnancy, and Special Needs

The following journey was never intended for publication. It was written from a mother, to her unborn child. The words detailed her struggle through infertility and the joy of finally being pregnant. A stunning revelation at her son's birth opened a world of both fear and discovery. This is the story of one mother's love and hope and...her quest for uninterrupted joy.

Now, enjoy bonus Chapters from Medieval Romance author Kathryn Le Veque's upcoming release, *SCORPION*. Kathryn is the author of over 60 Historical Romance novels. Find this novel, and many others, at all retailers. *SCORPION* will be released June 12, 2014.

PROLOGUE

Siege of Tripoli
March, 1289 A.D.
"Watch your head!"

The shout came from behind. The massive English knight with the shaved head instinctively took the hint and ducked low, missing being decapitated by mere inches. In spite of his size, the knight was as agile as a cat; he turned and charged the man who had just tried to remove his head from his shoulders, plowing a big shoulder into his attacker's belly.

The Mamluk warrior with the curved *kilij* sabre went down, flat on his back, and the enormous knight planted his big, heavy, straight-edge broadsword squarely into the man's chest. It was instant death.

"Kevin, we need to get out of here," the same knight who had shouted the warning was now grasping the arm of the big, shaved-headed knight. "This is a trap. They lured you here with rumors of an enemy surrender."

Sir Kevin Hage had realized the same thing his friend had; Tripoli had been under siege for over a month now, a bone-dry city in a dry and mysterious land. Overrun by Mamluks, Turks, Mongols, and more exotic tribes pouring in from the north and east, the last remnants of the Christian brotherhood in the Levant was trying to rid the city of the new legacy of invaders. But they were outnumbered; it had been a seemingly futile effort thus far.

Kevin and his companions, Sir Adonis de Norville and Sir Thomas de Wolfe, men he had grown up with and had now come to serve with in this strange and exotic land, the last crusade of an empire who had all but given up the quest, had been well out of England for over six years. From the snows of Wales to the searing sands of the Levant, it had all been quite an adventure, an adventure that has seen Hage acquire a reputation not only from those he fought with but from those he fought against. A man who fought with no fear, no emotion, and a hint of untapped vengeance. A man the Templars and Hospitallers alike had learned to use as a strike weapon, an assassin. Like a scorpion, Hage was often undetected until it was too late and by then, the target was dead before he realized what had hit him.

By then, it was too late....

Now, it was nearly too late for the man known as the Scorpion. Kevin looked around; they were on the north side of the city, having gained admittance by killing several gate guards at their post protecting a smaller but strategic postern gate that led into the walled city.

The lure of a possible surrender had drawn Kevin and his companions to the gate, as directed by the commander of the order of the Templars that Kevin sometimes fought with. Being English, and not officially a Templar or a Hospitaller, he fought with them when mood suited him, or when they would pay him well enough. Now, this directive he had received to collect surrendering enemy commanders, with a massive payment to boot, was coming to smell of an ambush. Already, their passage into the city had not been easy. Now he was wondering how easy it would be to get out.

"I believe you are correct," Kevin finally muttered, turning to Adonis; his tall, blond companion was red in the face from sun burn and heat. "De Clemont paid extraordinarily well for me to take on this task; it did not occur to me that it was because he knew he would eventually get his money back when my dead body was brought to him."

Adonis nodded, his expression edgy, as he motioned over Thomas de Wolfe, who had just dispatched two rather violent Mamluks. When de Wolfe kicked the bodies before stealing all he could carry off of them, he made his way back over to Kevin and Adonis.

"This is a trap," Thomas said; dark, with hazel eyes and big shoulders, he was one of the sons of the legendary William de Wolfe and possessed all of his father's great cunning and skill. His gaze was on Kevin. "If we venture further into the city where we have been directed to go, it will mean death for us. All of this…it has been far too planned."

"We know," Kevin murmured, looking around to see if any more assassins were about to pop from the shadows of the ancient city. "We must leave and leave quickly."

Adonis looked around him with the same hunted look that Kevin had. "We cannot return to de Clemont," he said. "The man put you in this position. If we return to him, then we return to our deaths."

Kevin knew that. He sighed heavily, wiping the sweat off his bristly scalp. "Not even those we have fought with for six years trust us any longer," he said. "If they are trying to kill us, then I believe our time here is done."

Thomas nodded, shoving the coinage he had stolen into the purse in his tunic. "They fear you are no longer under their control," he said. "You killed de Evereux…."

"He tried to kill me."

"Even so, rumor spread that you had been hired to kill him by the Mamluks."

Kevin grunted. "I killed the man because he was an unscrupulous French bastard who tried to steal some coinage from me," he said as if the entire thing was ridiculous. "When I confronted him, he tried to kill me. I killed him in self-defense."

Thomas knew that; so did Adonis. "But he was de Clemont's cousin," Adonis muttered. "Everyone knew he was an immoral fool but when you killed him, they sided with de Clemont out of fear of the man. One does not side against his leader and live to tell the tale."

Kevin was well aware. Clearing his throat softly, he looked around the dusty old walls of the antique city, walls the color of sand. Everything here was the color of sand; he hadn't seen green grass in over six years. At that moment, he realized that he missed it very much. He wanted to go home. He was tired of this place, its dirt and heat and lice. He wanted to see the green grass of home again.

"Then it is done," he said quietly. "We gather our possessions and we leave. We can do no more here and I refuse to lose my life on these barren sands, stripped of it by men who are unworthy of my legacy."

Neither Thomas nor Adonis argued with him; they, too, were glad to be leaving these desolate lands. They had only come because of Kevin, a man they had grown up with and a man who, six years ago, had lost the love of his life to another. Kevin had been aimless, directionless, and left with a massive hole in his chest where his heart used to be. At the request of Kevin's father, Sir Kieran Hage, Thomas and Adonis had stayed with Kevin and, at his side, had eventually found their way to the Holy Land in search of wealth and adventure.

But for Kevin, he was in search of something more, something to fill that big hole in his chest. The lost love had drained him of everything he had ever been capable of feeling and in that state, he became a mercenary for the Christian armies that were still trying to rid the Holy Land of the infidels. But he quickly found that there wasn't enough money to satisfy him or supply what he was lacking. Therefore, his early days as a mercenary transformed into something else, something dark and dangerous.

Kevin became a man who would take money to kill other men; it didn't matter who these other men were to him. As long as he was well-paid, he would do any task. Nothing was too great or too difficult. It was in this guise as a paid assassin that Kevin achieved something he never imagined he could. He became Death.

That hole in his chest where love used to linger was now filled by destruction and disappointment in what life had dealt him. The disillusionment of life had changed him, turning his soft heart and kind ways into a darker shadow of his former self. With dark hair shaved to the scalp and a massive tattoo of a scorpion that a Turkish artist has etched onto the left side of his back that had both terrible claws designed so that they were embracing his enormous left shoulder, Kevin Hage was no longer the pious, gentle knight those around him had known and loved. Kevin had died those six years ago and something else had taken his place.

The Scorpion was born.

"O thou noble maid! till I exalt myself to the heights of glory with the thrusts of my spear, and the blows of my sword, I will expose myself to every peril wherever the spears clash in the battle-dust—then shall I be either tossed upon the spear-heads, or be numbered among the noble in my quest for your beloved heart."

~ *13th Century Arabic Love poem*

ONE

London

October 1289

" **I** would like to know how the king even knows of me," Kevin said. "How on earth could he send word to see me?"

The question hung in the moist sea air. The cog that Kevin, Adonis, and Thomas had taken from Calais had come ashore at the white cliffs of Dover on a surprisingly mild fall day. The gulls hung in the sea breezes overhead as the knights, and several other passengers, disembarked as close to the shore as possible. Kevin disembarked with his horse, a spectacular white stallion he had purchased in Tyre, bred from the ancient Arabian stock crossed with the heavy boned Belgian warmbloods that the Crusaders had brought with them. The result was a smart, powerfully built, and astonishingly fast animal with a luxuriant dark gray mane and tail.

The horse could swim, too, among his many talents, so Kevin literally had the horse jump off the boat and swim to shore, which he happily did. Since no man other than Kevin could ride the horse much less approach it, Kevin simply followed his horse up onto the shore, grinning as the animal bolted up the rocky shoreline, kicking up his heels, before turning around and returning to his master. Like a dog, he followed Kevin obediently as the man took his baggage off the small skip they had lowered from the side of the cog.

This area of the shoreline was where boats from Calais disembarked so there was the usual amount of boat traffic and officials demanding tariffs. It smelled heavily of musty rocks and salt, the scent of the sea backed up against the cliffs. Bags in hand, Kevin stood before a man bearing the colors of Edward, the king, with the blue and red shield embracing golden royal lions, a messenger who seemed out of place among the salty seamen and aggressive tax collectors. The man had just informed Kevin of the king's wishes and Kevin was understandably confused.

"Rumor of your return to England precedes you, my lord," the messenger said. "All of England has heard of the Scorpion and our king, the consummate warrior, respects the reputation you have built for yourself. He wishes to see you for himself."

Kevin peered at the man dubiously. "How did you know me on sight?"

The messenger pointed to one of the several tariff collections milling several feet away, arguing with some of the cog captains that had come ashore.

"You are distinctive, my lord," he said, pointing to Kevin's neck. "Your boat captain noticed, too. If I was a man given to wager, I would guess those claws on your neck are scorpion claws. I *am* addressing the Scorpion, am I not?"

Kevin grunted; the right claw of the massive scorpion on his back came up on the left side of his neck. Instinctively, he ran a finger along the leather collar of his tunic as if trying to hide the claw that could not be hidden. There was no use in denying the obvious.

"I am Hage," he said, vaguely. "What does the king wish to speak with me about?"

The messenger was good at his job, seasoned and capable of standing up to me who were fearful, stubborn, or even intimidating. "He has not discussed that with me, my lord," he said. "I would suggest you travel to London immediately to find out. He is in residence at the palace at Thorney Island."

Thorney Island. Kevin turned to look at Adonis and Thomas, who were gazing back at him in various stages of confusion and perhaps even doubt at the messenger's words. But Kevin didn't doubt the man; he knew Edward's tunics. He'd seem them many times. Unless this was a spy who had stolen a royal tunic and was trying to lure him to his

186

death, at the palace at Thorney Island no less, he believed the man. He had no reason not to. Better not take the chance it that the king really had summoned him. Therefore, he waved the man off.

"Very well," he said. "If you reach the king before I do, tell him I am on my way."

The messenger bowed sharply. "Excellent, my lord," he said. "The king will be pleased."

With that, the man spun on his heel and took off across the rocking shore, dodging seamen and passengers alike as they disembarked from the cogs off short. As Kevin went to saddle his horse, Adonis followed him.

"Summoned by the king?" he repeated quietly, looking around at the rabble that was milling about on the shoreline to make sure no one had heard the messenger. "The last time you saw Edward was in battle in Wales and he believed you to be someone else."

Kevin put the saddle on his horse and adjusted the cinch strap. "I am well aware."

"He thought you were a Welsh insurgent."

Kevin nodded. "That is true," he said, thinking back to that dark night when he'd had a great adventure and a seriously close call against the king of England. "He thought that I was Bhrodi de Shera, the last hereditary king of Anglesey."

Adonis, too, thought back to that rather harrowing night of battle. "You donned the man's armor when he was wounded in battle so that the Welsh would not lose heart against the English," he muttered. "You did it because Penelope asked you to."

Kevin didn't want to think back to that part of the circumstances but he had no choice; even mentioning Penelope de Wolfe's name, six years later, still brought pain.

"I did it because she wished it," he murmured. "I did it because I loved her and I did not wish to see her miserable when her husband was wounded in battle. The deception nearly cost me my life."

Adonis nodded faintly; he glanced at Thomas as the man came upon them, listening to the conversation even as he was straightening out the knot of his horse's reins.

"I was there that night," Thomas put in. "Lest you forget, Kevin; I was there. I saw almost everything. Edward captured you and had it not been for my father and your father, you would have been in very serious trouble posing as an enemy Welsh prince, in front of the king no less. My sister should not have asked that of you. What will happen now when you show up to London and the king recognizes you?"

Kevin shrugged; he wasn't particularly concerned about it. He was more concerned about the fact that Penelope de Wolfe was on his mind now and he didn't want to be thinking about her the entire ride into London. *Damnation!* He thought angrily. It had taken him nearly every day of those six long years in the Levant to forget her; could a brief mention of the woman once he was on English soil undo all that had been done to erase her from his mind once and for all? He wondered.

"It was dark that night," he finally said. "I had more hair than I do now and was dirty, beaten, and dressed in another man's armor. I doubt the man will recognize me"

Thomas grunted in disapproval. "You are taking a terrible chance."

Kevin looked at him. "I do not have a choice," he said. "You saw for yourself; the king as summoned me. If I refused, I will be in greater trouble."

Thomas knew that but he still didn't like any of it. Shaking his head, he turned back to his big red steed and slid the bridle over the animal's big head. Adonis, too, was heading back to his horse even though his thoughts were lingering on the situation.

"Mayhap we should send for your father," he said. "It is possible we will need the man there when you meet with the king. Uncle Kieran can explain away what happened if, in fact, the king recognizes you."

Kevin shook his head. "I've not needed my father's help since I was a child," he said. "I will not call upon him now. If there is any reconciling to be done, I will do it."

"Aren't you going to send word to him anyway?" Adonis asked softly. "He will want to hear from you. I am sending word to my father right away, as is Thomas. If our fathers receive word from us and Uncle Kieran does not hear from you, he will worry and you know it."

Kevin was about to take a hard stance but thought better of it. After a moment, he nodded. "I will send word to him," he said, his gaze taking on a rather longing expression as his movements slowed. "I've not seen my father in six years. The last time I heard from him was three years ago and the missive from my mother said that my father was not in the best of health. I...I am almost afraid to send word to him, afraid of what I will discover."

Adonis and Thomas were thinking the same thing. "My father's health is good but he is older than God himself," Thomas said. "I last heard from him two years ago. He said that all was well and that he had more grandchildren now."

Adonis made a fact at Thomas as if the man had just said something terrible but Kevin knew what Thomas had meant.

"He meant from Penny," Kevin said, feeling that old familiar stabbing in his heart again. "As of three years ago, my mother said that she had at least two children. I am sure that she has had more by now."

They should have been my children, he thought even though he tried not to think those words. They came tumbling down upon him like boulders in an avalanche so he resumed saddling his horse, his movements quicker and more decisive now, as if trying to forget the impact of those thoughts. He was shaking off those boulders, one by one. Even though the events happened those six years ago, he still felt the impact of pain as if it was fresh.

Thomas and Adonis knew that but they kept silent. There wasn't much point in discussing the very issue that had seen him running off to the Levant. Therefore, they continued to saddle their horses in silence until Thomas pointed out another vessel that had come to lay anchor upon the rocky shores; it seemed that the boat was full of women, women that weren't all that well dressed, and the crewmen brought them ashore in a dilapidated dinghy. Once the women hit the shores, it was a screaming and shouting match with the tariff collectors and the women began to wail because they evidently didn't have the money to pay the taxes.

By that time, Kevin, Adonis, and Thomas were ready to leave and they did, leading their horses across the rocky ground, passing the howling women and the yelling tariff collectors, and past the general chaos of the beach area. The path led up a small incline to a larger road that led into the small village of Dover.

The massive, ancient castle was on the top of the bluffs to their right, up the white hill where some manner of fortress had been since Roman times. The sea breeze was picking up as they mounted their horses and headed into town, big white gulls following them as they headed into the heart of the berg. It was busy on this day with all of the travelers that had come ashore by boat, with people crowded in the street as they searched for lodgings. Still other people gathered in the church for prayer as vendors hawked unknown meat, burnt, and hot wine across the street. It was quite an active place as Kevin, Adonis, and Thomas made their way through it all.

"I will send word to my father that we have returned," Thomas said, looking around the bustling town. "Surely I can hire a messenger from among this rabble."

Kevin grunted. "Hiring a man is not the question," he said. "The question is if you can hire a reliable one. I am sure there are many men who would take your money and drink it away without taking a step towards the north of England."

Thomas continued to look at the people of the town as they passed them on their way out of the village. "Did you notice?" he asked. "Everyone has white skin. There are even a few people with red or blonde hair. And the hills are green. It is starting to occur to me that we are truly home."

Kevin looked around; the village was set between a series of hills, with the castle on a massive rise to the east. Everything was quite green, smelling of grass and damp and the salt of the sea. He took a long, deep breath, closing his eyes briefly to digest the smells. It did his hardened heart good.

"Indeed we are," he said. "I'd forgotten these scents. It smells of home."

Adonis was looking longingly at a tavern as they passed by. "And I have forgotten the taste of home," he said. "Could we not stop and remember just a few drops?"

Kevin grinned, glancing over his shoulder at the tavern built from the stones and timber. A painted sign nailed to the roofline proclaimed it to be the Gull and Piper, with someone having very badly painted the images of a gull and a piper. "It will take us at least two days to reach London," he said. "Do you really want to delay?"

Adonis nodded vigorously. "We have spent months traveling from the Levant," he said. "Let us at least sample a bit of English spirit now that we are on English soil."

Kevin couldn't deny him. He, too, was the least bit eager to sample home as well. Without another word, he turned his steed towards the inn. Adonis and Thomas eagerly followed.

The tavern was packed from the top of its slanted roof to the bottom of its uneven dirt floor. As the three knights pushed into the great common room, they could quickly see the amount of people jammed into the place. It smelled strongly of dirty bodies and urine. Kevin, not particularly long on patience and weary from the boat trip, began shoving people aside as he hunted for a table that would suit them. He spied one, over near the hearth, where four men were sitting. He didn't hesitate; he went straight to the table and grabbed the first man he came to.

"We require your table," he said, tossing the man aside and reaching for the second one. "Seek your rest elsewhere."

Adonis and Thomas began grabbing men as well and fairly quickly the entire table was vacant. They didn't sit down right away, however; like a dog guarding a bone, they stood with their backs to the table, daring any one of those four men to charge them. It was then that they realized they had not dislodged ordinary men – there was a lord and what appeared to be three guards. Kevin and his men could tell simply by the dress.

The lord was a very young man who was quite effeminate. In fact, he seemed to be wearing lip rouge. He was dressed in beautiful purple and red silks and it took Kevin a moment to realize that the young man had flowers in his hair. His entire aura was carefree and womanly, but the expression on the young lord's thin face was quite manly in its seriousness.

"By what right do you touch me?" he demanded. "I shall have you killed, do you hear?"

His expression may have been powerful but his voice sounded like a woman screeching. Kevin wasn't one to judge other men; he knew that he himself had become something of an oddity over the years, so he refrained from judging others. Each man had a story, he knew. Therefore, he faced the frilly young lord with a steady gaze.

"It is your right to try but I suggest that you do not," he said. "My companions and I have just reached England after returned home from the Levant. We require rest more than you do, so find another table."

The young lord flew at him, all slapping hands and screams. It was a temper tantrum, pure and simple, and when the young man drew near, Kevin reached out and pushed him away by his head. The young lord went sprawling and his guards put their hands to the hilt of their swords, but Kevin quickly held out a hand.

"I would not if I were you," Kevin said to the trio. "You will not survive. Take your lord and find another table."

The smell of a battle was in the air and the patrons of the tavern began to notice. In a herd, they began moving away from the conflict. The young lord, however, was still sitting on his bum, glaring up at Kevin in outrage.

"Do you not know who I am, you fool?" he yelled. "I am Roger Longespée, Viscount Twyford! That is correct; I am a viscount and my father is the Earl of Salisbury. My father will see that you are severely punished!"

Kevin didn't react other than to turn for the table. He sat, heavily, in one of the chairs but he made sure he was facing the viscount and his bodyguards. Then he picked up a half-full cup of ale and drained it.

The young viscount, seeing that his threat had no effect on the massive knight, picked himself out of the dirt, brushed off his silks, and once again approached Kevin. He lifted a hand to strike him but Kevin reached out, grabbed it, and promptly snapped bones.

The young viscount began screaming and his bodyguards charged. Kevin took out the first guard with a devastating blow to the face, collapsing the man's nose. As he fell away, Kevin lashed out a massive boot and kicked the second guard coming for him. The guard received a powerful kick to the gut and as he fell back, Kevin stood up and unsheathed his broadsword.

It was a heavy sword of the finest tempered steel and the blade had many hash marks on it; Kevin had taken up the habit a few years ago of marking his blade for every man he had killed on a sword that was as long as a man's arm. The steel, so far, had one hundred and sixty-three hash marks on it, carefully scratched on to the blade near the hand guard for the hilt. He did it as a reminder that someday, he could be a mark on another man's blade and he had no intention of his life becoming nothing more than a scratch on steel. Therefore, the weapon in his hand was more than something by which to take a life or defend it; it was his salvation in a sense. A reminder of his own mortality.

It was a reminder that was gleaming wickedly in the weak light of the tavern. As Adonis fended off the third guard, the second guard, the one that Kevin had kicked away, slashed at Kevin with his broadsword as Thomas vaulted over the table and went after the man. Now, was a vicious fight between the two of them as tables up-ended and the female patrons of the tavern screamed their fright. Kevin was watching Adonis make short work out of the third guard when he felt a sharp pain in his arm.

Quickly, he put a hand up to feel the pommel of a dirk sticking out of his upper left arm. Grabbing the dagger and yanking it out of his flesh, his fury surged as he turned to see the frilly young lord standing a few feet away, gasping gleefully at what he had done. But that glee turned to fury as he watched Kevin rip the knife out and throw it aside; now, the young lord quickly turned terrified as his attempt to injure the massive shaved-headed knight failed. As Kevin watched, the young lord reached down and unsheathed the sword of the guard whose face Kevin had destroyed. Now, armed with a heavy broadsword he was not accustomed to, he held it with both hands and aimed for Kevin's midsection.

Kevin fended off the first swipe, sending the viscount off-balance. Infuriated, the young lord brought the sword up again, both hands, swinging it with all his might. He missed Kevin by a wide margin but that didn't stop him from swinging again and still again. Kevin was able to easily deflect all blows. But seeing his lord in a fight, one of the viscount's men kicked Thomas aside and lunged at Kevin, nearly making contact. Kevin was distracted for a moment as he fought the man off. It was enough of a distraction for the young viscount to take another swipe at him with his sword. Seeing it out of the corner of his eye, Kevin did the only thing he could do; he defended himself. Ducking low to avoid being hit in the head with the tip of a sword, he came up from beneath the viscount's line of sight and plunged is broadsword straight into the young man's belly.

The viscount screamed as a very large sword pierced his abdomen. It was clear early on that it was a very bad wound because blood was literally pouring from the man's belly as an artery had been pierced. The young lord fell to the floor, howling, as he bled out all over the floor. His guards, distressed and injured themselves, yelled for help, calling for rags or moss or anything to stop the blood flow. Chaos ensued.

As the occupants of the tavern began to run about, some bolting for the door, Kevin quickly sheathed his sword and turned to his companions.

"We leave," he said, swiftly collecting his saddlebags from the table-top. "*Now.*"

Adonis and Thomas knew that tone; it wasn't meant to be disobeyed or questioned. Somehow, they often found themselves escaping volatile situations because Kevin truly didn't fight for the pleasure of it. He fought because it needed to be done. Now, he saw no need to remain in a tavern that was quickly deteriorating into pandemonium and, more than likely, more violence because of the viscount's death because his guards would seek vengeance for their foolish and immature lord. It would be their duty. Therefore, it was time once again to flee.

Onward to London and an audience with the king.

Made in United States
North Haven, CT
17 January 2022

14877397R00114